Tears s
as she laid he
allowing th
to sink into her heart.

Oh Lord, is there truly nothing else to be done? She bowed her head at the answer. Her uncle took her hand and squeezed it. As much as it hurt, she knew it was best for Scioto.

He flicked his eyes from hers to Peter's. "Take her inside."

"Sir," he said, his voice rough. "This is my fault, I should—"

"No, Peter. You're not for one second to believe that. You've taken better care of this horse than even I did when he first came to me. This happened for reasons known only to God. I've accepted that."

As he spoke, Scioto groaned. They approached the stall, and Anne watched as he struggled for a few moments then lay very still. Dr. Detmers felt for his pulse and shook his head. Scioto was gone.

Anne buried her face in her hands. Peter wrapped his arm around her waist, pulling her close, and she felt the warmth from his brow resting on the back of her head. Quiet filled the stable; the only sound was that of Dr. Detmers putting away his instruments.

JENNIFER A. DAVIDS

has lived in Ohio all her life and her family are long-time residents of the state. Her mother's side of the family is from central and southern Ohio, and her father has traced his side of the family tree back to the early eighteen hundreds. She is a graduate of The Ohio State University and feels blessed to have been called to a life of writing for the Lord. She lives in central Ohio with her husband and two children and is a member of ACFW. If she's not writing, she's reading, crafting, or watching a favorite movie or TV show—usually in that order!

Books by Jennifer A. Davids

HEARTSONG PRESENTS

HP960—*Yankee Heart*
HP975—*Wounded Heart*

Restored Heart

Jennifer A. Davids

Heartsong Presents

Thanks to everyone who has been praying for me, and a
big thanks to Max Lucado. Your books and UpWords helped
me through this book in so many ways. This book is dedicated
to Brian Arthur Carmen, my dear brother in Christ, fellow alumni
of The Ohio State University, and "i"-dotter for the
OSU marching band. I look forward to heaven,
when your presence will finally be restored to me.

A note from the Author:

*I love to hear from my readers! You may correspond with me
by writing:*

Jennifer A. Davids
Author Relations
P.O. Box 9048
Buffalo, NY 14240-9048

ISBN-13: 978-0-373-48626-7

RESTORED HEART

This edition issued by special arrangement with Barbour Publishing,
Inc., 1810 Barbour Drive, Uhrichsville, Ohio, U.S.A.

Chapter 1

Pittsburgh, Pennsylvania
May 1884

"I can assure you, Peter, I'm just as surprised as you."

Peter McCord stared at his uncle. Two months ago he was the most eligible bachelor in Pittsburgh society and the apple of his grandfather's eye. One month ago found him keeping vigil at the old man's bedside. A week ago he watched as Granddad was laid to rest, and less than a minute ago the words he'd just heard uttered left him speechless.

"There must be some mistake," he said, finally finding his voice. "Let me see the will."

Randall McCord rose from his seat behind the heavy walnut desk and handed the document to him. Peter took it and, rising from one of the leather chairs, crossed his grandfather's wood-paneled study to the window. He felt the blood leave his face as he took in Granddad's final words. He'd been left nothing, absolutely nothing. Peter's brow furrowed. "I don't understand," he muttered.

"I realize after my misunderstanding with my father you imagined he would leave everything to you—"

"Misunderstanding?" Peter locked eyes with his uncle. "I would hardly call nearly ruining everything Granddad worked for a 'misunderstanding'!" His uncle's eyes narrowed and Peter knew he'd struck a nerve. Uncle Randall's heavy-handed ways had almost run McCord Steel and Ironworks into the ground. The mill had lost a great deal of money and the workers had come close to rioting. Granddad had been beside himself with anger; so much so, he cut off his only son. "In light of that fact," Peter continued. "I'm the most logical choice as heir in spite of the fact that my interests lay elsewhere."

"Oh yes, your *interests*," his cousin Edward drawled, leaning against the bookcase behind his father. "Horse racing and chasing after every attractive young lady in the city."

"At least I have them to chase," Peter shot back. With his strong, handsome face, chocolate brown hair, and—as Granddad used to say—eyes greener than a spring meadow, Pittsburgh's eligible young ladies were more than willing quarry. Of course being Hiram McCord's heir didn't hurt either. "Tell me, how are your marriage prospects?"

A slow, smug smile grew over his cousin's face. "Much improved now that *I'm* heir of McCord Steel and you're—"

"That's enough." Uncle Randall glanced sharply at his son. "Peter, what exactly did you expect? Considering your disastrous time at Princeton—"

"I did graduate," Peter snapped, rereading the will carefully.

"Barely. You spent more time at the racetracks than attending to your studies. I'm sure my father realized you couldn't possibly oversee his fortune."

"Granddad knew I wouldn't run the mill like he did. He knew I had every intention of hiring the best possible man to oversee its operation."

"While you exhaust the McCord fortune on horses, I suppose."

"Granddad approved of my interest in horses. It was his idea to buy the farm in Ligonier—"

"Then why didn't he leave you even the smallest stipend to keep the farm running?"

Ignoring the question, Peter strode over to his uncle. "Granddad couldn't have left everything to you. He wouldn't have." He shook the document. "This can't possibly be the correct will. It must be an older version."

"It's the correct one, Peter," Edward said. "Didn't you check the date?"

Peter looked at the will again. It had been signed a little over a year ago. He put his hand over his eyes. What could he have done over the past year to cause his grandfather to do this? Why hadn't he at least warned him? Peter stiffened. That last night, before Granddad slipped away in his sleep, the old man had begged for his understanding when the will was read. Peter had thought it was the laudanum talking. He felt a hand on his shoulder. His uncle had risen from his seat and now stood next to him.

"It was my father's last wish that you be taken care of, and it is one I intend to honor," he said, his hand turning viselike.

Peter shook free, handed the will to his uncle, and walked to the door. "I'll take care of myself, thank you, Uncle Randall."

"And how will you manage to do that, may I ask?"

Peter turned. His uncle resumed his seat behind the desk.

"You've been left with nothing. Not even the smallest sum of money." Peter remained silent and he continued. "As I said, I am willing to support you, but there will be a few conditions."

"And those would be?"

"It's high time you used that education my father paid for. I assume you learned *something* in spite of your horrendous marks." His uncle's eyes narrowed keenly. "You will come to work for me at the mill and earn your keep for a change."

Peter smiled humorlessly and shook his head.

"My thanks for the offer, Uncle, but I have a very promising colt that will be ready to race soon. I think I'll take my chances with him. In the meantime, I'm sure Henry won't mind me staying with him." Peter knew he and his horse trainer would think of something to keep the farm running. Sell off a few mares perhaps— His uncle's voice stopped him in mid-thought.

"You could, if the farm still belonged to you."

Peter felt the blood leave his face. "What do you mean?"

"Despite the fact he bought it for you, it seems the farm is still in my father's name. Not yours. Therefore, it now belongs to me. I intend on dismissing Henry Farley and selling off the animals as quickly as possible."

Peter tried to digest what he'd just heard as his uncle moved swiftly on. "The other condition concerns Miss Leticia Jamison."

He looked at his uncle blankly. Leticia—Letty—was the daughter of his grandfather's lawyer, Simon Jamison. "What about her?"

"A month or so ago, you and she were invited to the club as guests of Mr. and Mrs. Braddock, were you not?"

"Yes." Nearly every young person of his acquaintance had been invited. Hazel Braddock had recently become engaged, and her parents arranged a sort of extended engagement party at the hunting and fishing club on Lake Conemaugh. Even as sick as he was, Granddad had insisted he go, eager for his grandson to make a match. Peter had been delighted to mingle with some fine young ladies from Harrisburg there, and even now, he couldn't help but smile at the memory of their charms. They had all but fallen over themselves, vying for his attention. How could they not? Uncle Randall cleared his throat and Peter blinked. "I'm sorry, did you say something?"

"I said, what exactly happened between you and Miss Jamison?" Uncle Randall asked.

"Nothing. If I hadn't rescued her, I doubt I would have talked to her very much the whole trip."

Letty was a sweet enough girl. Pretty, too, but not really Peter's type. Far too bookish for his tastes, she wasn't part of his circle of friends. She'd gone to school with Hazel, the only reason she'd been invited in the first place.

"Oh yes." His uncle shot his son a look. "You two took a walk and got lost, I believe?"

"Miss Jamison got lost," Peter corrected. "She'd never been to the lake before and wandered off by herself. We all went out looking for her, and I found her." And he'd been considered quite the hero by the rest of the young ladies as a result.

"I also heard she was hysterical when you brought her back."

"Well of course—she was out in the elements by herself for over an hour." Peter wished his uncle would get to the point. He needed to go to his room and figure out what he was going to do. If he could just get a few minutes to himself…but his uncle's next words jarred any other thought from his head.

"Her dress was ripped, almost beyond repair."

Peter frowned. "What are you implying?"

"Father's not implying anything," Edward said. "Letty says you took advantage of her."

"What? No!" That was a line he was always careful to not so much as approach—much less cross—no matter how tempting. The price, a wedding ring, was far too high. "She said she fell before I found her. She told everyone as much."

"To avoid any embarrassment, I'm sure," his cousin replied. "But she won't be able to explain the state she'll be in within a few months. Not without being married."

A sick feeling rose in Peter's gut as he realized he

had a bigger problem than simply being penniless. He looked from his uncle to his cousin.

"That can't be true. Nothing happened," he said.

"Her doctor has assured me that it is true."

"I'm *not* marrying Letty Jamison."

"Then you may leave this house at once. I'm sure my father would understand my refusing to abide by his last request considering the circumstances." A gleam appeared in Uncle Randall's eyes. "And if you think you have friends around here that will take you in, think again. One word of this will close every door in Pittsburgh. Considering your reputation, no one will doubt it for a moment."

Peter felt all control of his world slipping away. It must have shown on his face, judging by his uncle's next words.

"Your aunt will help her with the arrangements. Since we are in mourning, the wedding will happen quietly in the parlor in a month's time. I think you'll agree we shouldn't wait any longer—for Miss Jamison's sake."

One month later, Peter shrugged reluctantly into a linen shirt and buttoned it, while his valet sorted through his cufflinks.

"The mother-of-pearl set will do fine, Jimmy."

Though surprised, he did as he was told. A knock at the door interrupted them. Setting the links aside, Jimmy walked over to answer it. Peter scowled as he heard him speak a few murmured words. What on earth did Uncle Randall want from him now?

Jimmy returned, a velvet box in his hand and an

uneasy look in his eyes. "Your uncle sent this up. He says it's a gift...for her."

Peter opened it. A pearl necklace lay inside, and not just any piece of jewelry.

"This belonged to my mother." He clenched his jaw. His uncle had taken charge of it when he had Peter's things moved from his spacious room on the floor below to this small, cramped, forgotten room in the garret. "And he expects me to give it to Letty?" He snapped the box shut. "He can go straight to the devil!"

Peter slapped the box down on his desk and snatched up his cufflinks. He fumbled with them, trying to put them on. Jimmy quickly came to his aid. Poor Jimmy. He was valet to Edward now, but Peter had insisted the young man be permitted to help him dress one last time. He needed a friend close by on the day he would lose what little freedom still remained to him.

"Thank you, Jimmy. I'm sorry I sounded short."

"It's all right, sir," the young man said as he handed Peter his tie.

"I'm sorry, too, for all this. My cousin can't be very pleasant to work for." Peter couldn't help but smirk as he fashioned a perfect four-in-hand knot. "Although, I have to admit I am pleased every time I see one of your sad knots hanging around his neck."

Jimmy gave him a self-conscious smile. Tying cravats and ties was the young man's only failing as a valet, but Peter had never minded.

"And he thought you were the master behind my perfectly formed ties," he said.

"Yes, sir, thank you for keeping that secret for so long." He helped Peter into his frock coat and brushed imaginary dust from the shoulders. As Peter made some final adjustments, Jimmy picked up the velvet case. "May I, sir?"

Peter nodded and watched him open the case and look admiringly at the necklace inside. It was the only thing of his mother's Peter owned. Granddad had given it to him several years ago, and he remembered that moment as the sole time his grandfather ever mentioned her. Even then, it was only to say that she had been a lovely young woman. The sadness in his face and eyes had kept Peter from pressing him for more. Sarah McCord's death had been tragic; a carriage accident had taken the life of Granddad's only daughter. Peter's father divorced and abandoned his mother before his birth, which was why he bore the name McCord.

"If you'll pardon the cheek, sir, it's not right for Miss Jamison to have this." He set it back on the desk then walked to the window and peered out.

Jimmy had been the only one to believe his assertion that nothing had happened between him and Letty. He'd been as outraged at her claim as Peter had, if not more. Peter smiled humorlessly. "Don't apologize; you're right. But as much as I agree with you, I don't think I have much choice in the matter."

He joined him at the window. A starling flitted from one bush to another in the gardens that lay directly below them. He envied the bird's freedom. Peter's every move had been closely monitored for the past month. He felt as if he were being kept in a deep hole, only to be taken out when needed. Almost sick with anger, he turned away from the window and ran frustrated hands through his hair. Spying the velvet case, he opened it and carefully removed the pearls. They shimmered gently in his hands, and the ornate clasp glittered. Bile rose in his throat as he imagined them around Letty's neck. He glanced at Jimmy.

"Who brought the necklace up here? Jenkins?" His uncle had fired Martin, their old butler, when he and his family came to live at the McCord mansion, and elevated one of the older footmen to his position. Albert Jenkins, a sharp-eyed man, reported Peter's every move to his uncle.

"No, sir, it was one of the maids. Jenkins is sick as I understand it."

Opportunity whispered in Peter's ear. Laying the necklace on the desk, he sat down and pinched the bridge of his nose. "Would you mind getting me something to drink?"

"Of course, sir. Anything in particular?"

"Something that will get me through the rest of the day." He looked at him with raised eyebrows and Jimmy smiled and nodded before leaving the room.

With one fluid motion, Peter pulled out pen and paper, scribbled a note to the valet, and then placed the envelope where only Jimmy would find it. Glancing at himself in the mirror, he traded the frock coat for his sack suit jacket and quickly dispensed with his tie and collar. That was better. He looked a little more working class now. There was only one thing to be done, only one way out, and he intended to take it. He went to the door, down the back stairs, out the servant's door, and on his way to the section of Pittsburgh that boasted the most pawnshops.

Chapter 2

Ostrander, Delaware County, Ohio
September, 1884

Anne Kirby pulled her trunk from the corner where it sat, over to her bed and raised the lid. She stared at it for a long moment, and then bit her lip, trying to set her mind on preparing for her trip. But her wandering thoughts tumbled like jagged rocks in her mind, and a headache began to prick behind her brown eyes. Closing them, she sat on the edge of her bed, not hearing her mother come in.

"Are you all right?"

The lilt of her mother's German accent and the gentle pressure of her hand on her shoulder startled Anne. She looked up, a smile flickering across her face as she rose. "I'm fine, Ma. I was just…thinking."

"Why is your trunk out?"

"I thought I might pack a few things." She walked over to her wardrobe and began taking her things out and laying them on the bed. She felt her mother's eyes on her as she knelt in front of the trunk. "I'll need some paper."

"Anne, you do not leave for a week, yet." She held out her hand to her daughter. "Sit with me for a moment."

Anne paused then took her hand. They sat on the bed and her mother brushed a thumb across her cheek.

"I do not like to see you hurt."

Anne nodded, her gaze directed at her lap. Her mother grasped both her hands and squeezed them.

"I'm sorry Sam McAllister treated you as he did. He shouldn't have courted you if he had feelings for another. Your pa was ready to go up there and give him a piece of his mind."

Anne glanced up. "He was? Does he still have a mind to do that?"

"No, *kleine,* I convinced him not to go. He promised me he wouldn't."

"Good. I would just as soon forget the whole thing." Her heart pounded with relief. She wished she could forget those months she had taught school in the northern part of the county. Everything had looked so promising, at first. She brushed a strand of ginger-colored hair from her eyes before changing the subject. "Ma, don't you think I'm a little old for you to still call me 'kleine'?"

Her ma smiled and gently touched her chin. "Don't you know no matter how old you are, you will always be my 'little one'?"

Anne grinned lopsidedly. It was still appropriate, she supposed. She was the shortest one in the family. Even her younger sister, Millie, was an inch or so taller than she.

Her mother cupped her face. "Besides, calling you kleine always reminds me of that special day."

"The day you found me," Anne said.

Her ma nodded and wrapped her arms around her. Barely three at the time, Anne remembered only snatches of what had happened, like the purple flowers she'd hidden behind, and the kindness in Ma's blue eyes as she coaxed her to come closer. And seeds. Ma had been planting the kitchen garden and convinced her to help. But the gentle memory contrasted sharply with the hard truth. She formed her next words carefully.

"I wish I knew exactly when my birthday is and how old I really am." Anne pulled away and scrutinized her mother's face. The barest hint of apprehension slipped across the older woman's face before a gentle smile settled there.

"I know, kleine. But your parents were already gone when we found you." She rose and looked from her daughter to the clothes on her bed. "I suppose we can pack some of your winter things. It will save time, later. I'll get some newspaper."

While she was gone, Anne carefully folded her skirts and waists. She'd always known she was adopted—everyone in Ostrander knew—but she hadn't known there was more to it until recently.

Your parents were already gone....

She winced at the half-truth. For a moment, her clothes faded from sight and clear, precise handwriting flashed before her eyes, words never meant for her to see. Her brows angled, *V*-shaped, above her eyes, and she squeezed them shut, swallowing her desire to tell Ma what she knew. What good would it do to say something now? Telling her parents she knew the truth would only hurt them, and most certainly keep her from carrying out her plans. After all, it was only after Anne made certain concessions that they agreed to let her leave. She wondered if she still wanted to go through with it. *No, this has to be done.* At least, no one else in Ostrander appeared to know. And if things went as she hoped, they never would. Her thoughts gave her hands urgency, and she reached for the quilt at the end of her bed and folded it. Her mother returned to the room.

"Ah, you're taking your quilt." Ma stood beside her. "I remember when I made this for you. You helped me—do you remember?"

"Yes, I remember pricking my fingers so many times I left a drop of blood on it." She smiled as she lifted a corner of the quilt to reveal the tiny brown dot that never fully washed out.

Her mother carefully laid it over the heavier items already packed in the bottom of the trunk. "We'll miss your help around here."

Anne chuckled ruefully. "I'm not that useful. That's why I became a teacher, remember?"

If her parents hadn't told her she was adopted, she would have figured it out on her own. Pa and her brother, Jacob, could sow crops in seawater and they would grow. Her ma ran the farmhouse with an efficiency that, according to Pa, would be the envy of any army drill sergeant. And Millie's needlework had won more first place premiums at the county fair than Anne could count. She, on the other hand, couldn't sew, burned water, and the last time she had charge of the kitchen garden, everything nearly died.

"You will still be missed, Anne." Adele, her hands on her hips, looked at her. "Although, I still don't see why you must leave or why you're going to work in the library at The Ohio State University. You are a teacher."

"I wanted a change. And there were no positions available for me in Columbus, at least, not right now." Anne avoided her gaze and laid a waist into the trunk. "The young lady I'm filling in for is supposed to return in a few months, maybe by that time—"

"Anne." Her mother squeezed her arm. "I know what happened with Sam was hard, but why can't you stay?"

Anne looked down at the things in her chest, the real reason nearly flying from her lips. "Ma, I—" She took a breath. "I need to do this." She looked up at her mother with pleading eyes.

Her ma wrapped her arms around her. "We will pray for you, kleine, that God will heal your heart to love again."

"Thank you," Anne murmured then gently pulled away and walked over to the wardrobe. She made a play of looking for any forgotten items while attempting to swallow the lump in her throat. Her parents had never pushed her to get married, but she sensed they were eager for her to find a match soon. At twenty-one, most young women her age had been married for a few years. It wasn't that she didn't want to marry nor

that she lacked beaus—she'd simply never found someone she felt she could walk alongside for the rest of
her life. She had always trusted God would lead her to
that person when the time came and, until a few weeks
ago, she thought that person had been Sam McAllister.
Now she had to wonder if there really was anyone for
her to call her own. Composing herself, she picked up
a forgotten shawl.

"I am glad you will not be on your own down in Columbus," her ma said as she approached. "Your uncle
will take good care of you."

"Yes." Anne folded the garment. When she first told
her ma and pa of her plan to work at the university's
library, they had given her their consent, but only if
she lived with Uncle Daniel, a professor at the institution. They simply wouldn't hear of her living at one of
the boardinghouses near the school, even if they did
cater exclusively to the female students. At first, she
thought it would be a problem, but then she realized
she would not have to pay for her room and board. That
would make saving her money for passage west all the
easier. She laid the shawl in the trunk. "That's all my
winter clothing."

"We can pack the rest later." Ma closed the lid.
"Let's go see how Millie is doing with dinner."

They made their way out behind the house to the
summer kitchen. Although Anne didn't cook, she
managed to help out by fetching and carrying various
things her mother and sister needed.

"I'm rolling out the dough now, Ma," Millie said
as they came in.

"The dough for what?" Anne inhaled the fragrant

chicken boiling in a large pot on the black cast iron stove. "Oh Ma, you shouldn't be going to such trouble."

"Yes, I should. I couldn't have you leave without making your favorite dishes."

"Tonight we're having chicken pie, green beans, fresh bread, and Ma's strudel for dessert." Millie smiled broadly and brushed a strand of her bright blond hair from her face.

Tears caused Anne's sight to swim for a moment. Blinking them away, she took a basket from the work table. "I'll go pick the green beans."

"I've already done it."

"Is there anything for me to do just now?" Anne asked hopefully.

Ma looked at her and then sighed. "No. You can go on out to the barn."

She smiled. "Thank you, Ma."

Anne stepped inside the barn and breathed in the familiar, earthy odor of weathered wood, hay, and straw. It was one of her most favorite places. She missed the days of her childhood when she would follow Pa from the hay maw above to the milking stalls down below, helping him and the hired hands tend the livestock. But as she grew older, Pa told her she shouldn't be hanging around the barn so much. Learning to take care of a home, not animals, was more important, he'd said. She found it a little ironic that the one thing she felt gifted to do on the farm was the one thing that wasn't proper for her to do. At least Pa had allowed her a little leeway lately. A soft nicker greeted her approach to the horse stalls. A dark head with a graying muzzle appeared, and Anne smiled, drawing from her pocket the carrot she had snitched from one of the feed bins.

"Hello, Scioto," she said, dropping it into his feed trough, glad that the horse would be coming with her.

Scioto belonged to Uncle Daniel. He leased a house on university grounds and Pa had been boarding him while the university built a stable on the property. The horse finished the carrot and looked to her for more. She smiled as she scratched his withers, a favorite spot.

"That's enough for now, boy." Pa had left his care to her since she came home, and she had become attached to the horse over the past few months. The bay Morgan nuzzled her and she stroked his neck.

"I hear you started packing your trunk. I don't suppose Ma was able to talk you out of leaving."

Anne turned to see Pa approach. She smiled apologetically, shaking her head. He sighed and wrapped his arms around her, bending his tall form as he did so.

"How's my Annie?"

"I'll be all right."

She felt his arms tighten and knew he still struggled not to go confront Sam. A mixture of panic and guilt surged through her. What if he did? He would certainly find out that Sam had not led her on as she had allowed her parents to believe. *No, he promised Ma,* she told herself. *And he never breaks his promises, especially to her.* While the thought eased the panic, it did little to assuage her guilt, and the urge to blurt out the truth once again enveloped her. She bit her lip and clung to Pa. How she would miss his hugs and the way he called her "Annie." He was the only person in the whole world allowed to call her that. Scioto snuffed at them, demanding attention, and Anne's throat loosened as she laughed softly.

"This horse sure has become attached to you." Pa released her to face the animal. "I hope he eats for whoever Danny hired."

"So it won't be me?" It was silly of her to ask, she knew, but she had hoped, since she'd been allowed to take care of him here—Pa laid a gentle hand on her shoulder.

"I only let you take care of him when you came home because it seemed to make you feel better, but it won't be fitting for you to see to him down there. You let the stable boy see to him."

"Yes, Pa." She stroked the horse's neck. If she didn't take care of him, who would she talk to? Scioto had become her sole confidant. Well, she could still go visit him—in the evenings, maybe.

"Besides, all those young men down there won't want you smelling like horse," he added.

Anne said nothing and fussed with Scioto until Pa took her by the chin, forcing her to look up at him.

"I know it's hard, but trust God with your heart and your future."

Anne swallowed the words impossibly stuck in her throat. It wasn't about trust. Not really. She trusted that God knew what He was doing. She just couldn't understand why. With Pa's gentle eyes still watching her, she tried to form a reply. The gentle low of a cow told her it was time to do the milking.

"The cows are waiting," she said.

"I'd best go let them in," Pa said slowly. "Think on

what I said." She nodded, and he gave her a quick hug then turned to leave.

Once he was gone, Anne fetched a brush and stepped into Scioto's stall to groom him. The swish of the brush as it smoothed his coat usually had a soothing effect on her. But packing her trunk today had nudged her plans into motion, like the wheels of a train pulling from the station. She leaned against the horse's shoulder, and he gently snuffed and nuzzled her. She shed a few tears into his mane then dashed them away when Pa came in to do the milking.

It was the ache in his head that woke Peter more than the fact he was comfortable for the first time in months. He raised his hand to his head then opened his eyes when it came in contact with a bandage. The images around him were blurry at first, and he blinked to clear his vision. It was dark outside, and the low lamplight glowed softly over the room. He was in a bed with clean sheets and, judging from the feel of the cloth against his skin, clean clothes as well. Raising himself up on one elbow, he tried to look beyond the edge of the soft pools of light. The room was small but nicely furnished. So much so, he wondered if he was back in Pittsburgh. As his eyes adjusted, he could just make out a man's form in a chair near the foot of the bed. His heart started and he spoke without thinking. "Granddad?"

The man chuckled. "No, I'm not quite that old."

"I'm sorry," Peter said.

"Don't be; I'm sure to be called that someday, just not quite yet." He leaned into the light. Round spectacles sat on a slender face, which the lines of age were clearly beginning to march across. His dark blond Van Dyke beard and mustache were shot with a generous amount of gray, as was his hair, which was swept back and to the side. He had a reassuring smile on his face. "I'm Professor Daniel Kirby. Who might you be?"

"Peter," he replied then looked down at the bed-clothes. "Peter…Ward." He'd dispensed with his real name long ago, but it still felt strange saying the new one aloud. Ward had been his father's last name. The way Peter saw things, it was time the man who sired him contributed something to his life, seeing how he'd never wanted anything to do with him while he was growing up.

The professor was silent for a moment. "I see. We'll let that be for now. What do you remember?"

Peter closed his eyes against the onslaught of memories the question evoked. One foolish decision had made him utterly homeless, and he'd been tramping his way around three different states in as many months. He'd gained a few friends as he eked out an existence, but it was still a lonely and often dangerous way of life. He remembered hopping a boxcar in Cincinnati and drifting off to sleep. The next thing he knew, he heard yelling and felt hands taking hold of him. "I remember being pulled off the train by a group of boys. They forced me to run between two rows of them while they tried to hit me with sticks." He could feel the lump on his head through the bandage. "I guess I didn't do too well."

Professor Kirby nodded. "It's called a 'timber lesson,' an education young boys and—I'm sad to say—

some grown men like to give tramps." He shook his head. "It all comes from too much freedom in the home. Boys raised like that seldom end well." Peter winced slightly and the professor, his face full of concern, asked, "Are you in pain?"

"No, not really." The truth of those words had stung, though. In the past months, he'd been forced to look his own lack of guidance square in the eye.

"The Lord was surely looking after you today. It had to have been His hand that guided my colleague, Professor Townshend, and me to pass that alley when we did. We put a stop to it, but not before you took quite a blow to the head." The professor stood and gently forced Peter to lay back. "Professor Townshend also happens to be a medical doctor. He says you should stay in bed for a few days."

"Then, I suppose, you'll send me off to the poorhouse." Sighing, he laid his arm over his eyes. He'd spent one night in a poorhouse and swore never to do so again. He'd been shocked to see people placed in such deplorable conditions just because they were poor.

"No."

The professor's decisive tone surprised Peter, and he lifted his arm to look at him. His face was just as firm as his voice had been.

"I'm curious about your clothes." Professor Kirby nodded to where they lay, across the back of a chair next to the bed.

Peter's heart began to pound. They were worn and dirty, but not nearly enough for someone not to see their quality.

"The sack suit jacket seems appropriate enough.

But where does a man like you get such finely made shirt and pants?"

Peter swallowed and looked away. He already liked this man and didn't want to lie to him. But how could he tell him the truth? Meeting his eyes, he settled for partial truth. "I didn't steal them."

There was a pause then Professor Kirby nodded. "I believe you." His gaze dropped and Peter just made out what he said next. "Looking at you, how can I not?" With a slight shake, he roused himself, raised his eyes, and smiled slightly. "We'll leave the other mysteries about you for later. It's late and you should rest."

"Sir?"

The professor looked back as he opened the door.

"Where am I?"

"You're in my home. On the grounds of The Ohio State University in Columbus, Ohio. Try to sleep now." The door closed quietly behind him.

But Peter lay awake. How would he explain the mysteries about himself to this man who had so kindly taken him in, at least for the moment?

Too much freedom in the home.

The words echoed in the walls of his heart, their truth tearing at him. Forced to beg for food and shelter had humbled him, considerably. He'd come to see how spoiled he was. Earning your food was much different from having it set in front of you by a servant every night. No wonder Granddad had been angrier about Uncle Randall's cuts in the worker's wages than about the money McCord Steel had lost under his uncle's care. He'd seen more than his share of youngsters homeless because their families couldn't afford to feed them. Saddest of all were those who couldn't hold a job because something was wrong with them—their mind or body had been injured and work wasn't possible.

As Hiram McCord's grandson, he'd always thought himself too good to have to earn his keep. He didn't think that way now. His uncle had been right, at least on that score: high time he earned his way in the world. The irony of it all was now that he wanted to work, he couldn't find a job—one look at him and no one wanted to hire him. The professor was the first person in a long time to see the man, not the tramp.

The Lord was surely looking after you today.

Professor Kirby was clearly a man of faith. He said those words as if he'd been speaking of a friend. If anyone would be willing to help him find an honest job, it was him. He just hoped he wouldn't have to tell the professor any more about his past than necessary. At least he'd believed him when Peter said he hadn't stolen the clothes.

He found the man's faith curious. Peter had never met someone who actually followed what the Bible commanded. He certainly hadn't done so, nor had anyone else in his acquaintance. For appearance's sake, Granddad had made him go to church every week without fail, and as a result, he'd taken to seeing God as nothing more than someone he had to listen to once a week. As sleep finally began to melt over him, he wondered if there might be more to God than just that.

Chapter 3

"You've decided to keep the beard."

Peter looked up from his breakfast to find Dr. Kirby scrutinizing him. It had been a week and a half since he'd been brought to the professor's home. He was up and about now, and although he'd made some changes to himself, the beard hadn't been one of them.

"Mrs. Werner tried to get me to shave it again this morning, but I told her I've decided to keep it." He smiled, remembering the housekeeper's less than enthusiastic reaction.

"I'm a little…surprised," the professor replied. "I never liked having a beard when I was your age."

Peter thought he sounded disappointed. In all honesty, he'd have rather been clean shaven, but the thought that his uncle might be looking for him was enough to decide otherwise.

"At least I look a little more presentable now. I can't

imagine why you bothered with me, looking as I did."
He'd been shocked to see himself in the mirror a few
days ago, when Mrs. Werner gave him a trim. His
hair and beard had grown considerably in the three
months he'd been on the road. "I must've looked like
a wild man."

"You were still a man, Peter. And in God's eyes,
you were worth the bother. Don't you remember our
discussion about Zacchaeus, yesterday?"

Peter nodded. That, and many other discussions,
had been born out of his attempt to keep all conversation away from himself. Professor Kirby had been
only too happy to talk about God, but Peter sensed he
saw through his ploy. While that, indeed, may have
been his plan at first, by his second or third day in bed,
Peter began to feel a hunger for God he hadn't known
before. The professor's kindness tapped something in
his heart, and he drank up all the professor told him
and eagerly read the Bible he'd lent him.

"It doesn't matter who you are in man's eyes. God
looks at the heart." Dr. Kirby's expression grew wistful. "That was one of my wife's favorite verses. First
Samuel 16:7: 'For man looketh on the outward appearance, but the Lord looketh on the heart....' "

Peter watched him, concerned. While he'd managed to reveal little about himself, Dr. Kirby shared
much about himself and his family. He still felt keenly
his wife's death over a year ago. "Professor? Are you
all right?"

"I was blessed to have my Katherine for the years I
did." Dr. Kirby roused himself. "She's with God now,
celebrating the decision you made a few days ago."

Peter smiled. His second day out of bed had been fine, and he and the professor went for a walk. Dr. Kirby led them alongside a spring until they came to what the student body called simply The Lake, nestled in a tree-lined vale. On its shores, their conversation turned quite serious. And Peter decided to clothe himself with Christ.

But his excitement of feeling right with God was dampened because he couldn't bring himself to tell Dr. Kirby his whole story. He couldn't bear the thought of the disappointment in the doctor's eyes when he told him about the ugly person he had once been. He could hardly think of it himself. Maybe it would be best if he moved on as quickly as possible. But how? He didn't have a job. He didn't even own the clothes he now wore. He looked at the professor.

"Thank you for giving me these clothes, sir. I'll return them to you when my own are clean."

"Keep them. I insist."

Peter bit his lip. However much had been spent on him, he was determined to pay back.

They finished their breakfast, or rather, Peter did. Professor Kirby had been eating until he mentioned his wife. After that he'd allowed the rest to grow cold, between reading the *Columbus Dispatch* and staring out the window. He revived somewhat when he discovered Peter intended to spend time reading his Bible and invited him into the library.

"Classes will begin soon, and I have lecture notes and lessons to review. It will be nice to have company for a change."

The library connected to the parlor through a set of

sliding doors, which were open. While the professor
settled behind his desk, Peter found himself drawn to
the pictures on the oak mantel.

"Are these of your family, sir?"

"Yes," Dr. Kirby replied. "Please, feel free to look
at them."

The first was a photograph of two young people,
only a few years younger than he. "Are these your
children?"

"Yes. Rebecca and Joseph. She's married and lives
in Cincinnati. My son is in college—in Maine."

Noting the slight pause, Peter looked closely at Joseph. Was his relationship with the professor strained?
He thought better of asking, especially after noticing
the pensive look that crossed the professor's face before he turned his attention to the papers before him.

The next pictured a lovely dark-haired woman sitting on a chair, the professor standing behind her. It
was, without a doubt, a picture of him and his wife,
taken several years ago. They both looked so young.
Peter now understood, if only a little, Professor Kirby's
pain. The look of kind serenity on Katherine Kirby's
face was enough to assume she must have been a gentle
and gracious woman. In some hazy way, she reminded
him of his own mother. He had vague memories of her
having that same sweet look on her face, and dark hair
as well. Peter moved to the next picture, and his eyes
widened at the vision.

It would be nothing short of an insult to call the
young woman merely pretty, at least to Peter's way of
thinking. As far as he was concerned, she was the most
beautiful thing he had ever seen. The black and white

photograph made it impossible to tell exactly the color of her hair, but her ringlets shone smooth, and her large eyes were lively above a small, straight nose and pert mouth. The more he looked at her, the more fascinated he became, and he immediately began to plan how to win her over. Every girl was different. Some required gifts, others responded to effusive compliments. He'd even attended a temperance meeting in order to win one young lady's affections. Some girls were hard to crack, and some were ridiculously easy, but one way or another, they always laid their hearts at his feet. Certainly, she would be no different.

"That's my niece, Anne."

He started but covered it by quickly turning his head toward the professor. "Your brother's daughter?" He hoped he spoke loudly enough to drown out the pounding of his heart.

"Yes, that's him in the next picture over."

Peter turned to see the professor's wedding picture. Two other men were in the photograph besides Dr. Kirby. One smiled jovially, the other looked angry and surly. Just as he was hoping the pleasant man was the young lady's father, the professor spoke again. "I'm sorry he looks so cross. Jonah didn't feel himself that day."

Peter's heart now pounded twice as hard. He took another look at Jonah Kirby, feeling sure the man somehow knew what he'd been thinking about his daughter. He looked down at the stonework on the fireplace, guilt bearing down on him like a steel beam. How could he think that way about the professor's niece, or any young lady for that matter? Hadn't his near miss with Letty taught him anything? And on the road, how many times had he watched men charm young women into committing deplorable things for them? His thoughts added more weight to the guilt he already felt. He should be ashamed of the way he'd treated the fairer sex. Letty included.

"They'll be arriving next week." Peter almost didn't hear the words. He looked up as they fully registered.

"They will?"

"My niece is coming here to live with me. She'll work in the university library." He rose and joined him at the mantel. "Their arrival brings me to something I wanted to discuss with you." Apprehension must have shown on Peter's face because Dr. Kirby smiled and patted him on the shoulder. "Don't look so alarmed; I have no intention of putting you out. Quite the opposite." He took his arm. "Let me show you something."

Peter followed the professor through the dining room and kitchen, and out the back door. They walked to the northwest corner of the fenced lot, where a brand-new stable had been erected.

"My brother has been taking care of my horse, Scioto, while the university had this built." Dr. Kirby opened the door and they walked in. As Peter breathed in the smell of fresh wood, straw, and feed, a host of other memories assailed his thoughts. A deep longing for his own stables rose in his heart. But he quickly dashed it against the hard fact that his love of horses had cost him dearly. *Remember the racing park in Pittsburgh? You wouldn't be homeless now if you hadn't placed all your money on that "sure thing."*

"Jonah will bring Scioto with him when he brings

my niece," the professor said. "I'd like for you to stay and take care of him. I don't know what your background with horses is, but I was brought up on a farm, and I'm more than willing to teach you all I know."

Peter took in the hopeful look on the professor's face and then looked around the stable. The offer was the chance he'd been hoping for; a job which would pay wages, giving him the ability to earn his keep. But, considering his past, could he trust himself to take it?

Anne was worried about her uncle.

As they sat at the breakfast table, she couldn't help noticing that, once again, he'd ignored the food Mrs. Werner prepared. Oatmeal, eggs on toast, and the remainder of her mother's strudel remained untouched. The oatmeal's presence meant Mrs. Werner worried about him as well. She had to have gotten up quite early to make it. Coffee was all he'd consumed between reviewing notes for his first class and reading the *Dispatch*. She eyed the strudel, truly surprised he hadn't taken even a bite. It was one of his favorites. Ma had sent it with her, having made it specifically for him. But in the few days since she arrived, Anne had eaten most of it.

Since her aunt's death, he hadn't been the same, but she didn't recall him behaving quite like this. She used to see her uncle more often, when he lived just east of the farm in Delaware and taught at Ohio Wesleyan. Since starting at The Ohio State University, contact between him and her family was limited to weekly letters and holiday visits, and he'd always seemed reasonably cheerful. Over his shoulder, she caught a glimpse of

Mrs. Werner opening the kitchen door a crack. Anne shook her head, and the housekeeper, pressing her lips together, returned to the kitchen. Anne rose from her seat and took up her dishes.

"Can I get you more coffee, Uncle Daniel?"

He looked up from his notes and smiled. "No, thank you, Anne. You can take my dishes. I'm finished."

She looked at him reprovingly. "Uncle Daniel, you haven't eaten anything."

"I'm not very hungry this morning."

Anne sighed and set all the dishes on the tray Mrs. Werner had left on the side table. She lifted it and carefully backed her way through the swinging door leading to the kitchen.

"He will waste away to nothing if he keeps eating so." Mrs. Werner took the tray from Anne. " 'Tis true he never ate much since I came to work for him, just after Mrs. Kirby died, God rest her soul, but since young Mr. Ward left—"

"Mr. Ward? Who's he?"

"Ah, I thought he had told you about him. A week before you arrived, Dr. Kirby went into town with Professor Townshend. They happened upon this young man being beaten in an alley and brought him back here." She washed the dishes and Anne dried them with a dishcloth.

"Why was he being beaten?"

"He was a tramp. Some young boys thought it was good sport."

"How barbaric! Was he badly hurt?"

"No, although Dr. Townshend did have him stay in bed for about a week. Dr. Kirby took a shine to him though. Spoke to him about the good Lord and young Peter took it to heart." Mrs. Werner handed Anne the last plate and wiped her wet hands on her apron. "He offered him a job looking after his horse, but Peter turned him down. Ever since he left, Dr. Kirby's been distracted and melancholy."

Anne's brow furrowed as she put the dried dish in the cupboard. "That's odd. Did my uncle say why he turned the offer down?"

"No, but he had the coloring of your cousin, Joseph." She gave Anne a knowing look.

It made sense now. Her cousin was one of the reasons Uncle Daniel decided to teach at the university. Joseph had decided to attend the university, but just a few months before he was to start, Aunt Kitty passed away. He'd abruptly decided to switch schools and instead left Ohio to attend Bowdoin College in Maine. Her uncle missed his son dearly.

Anne sighed. "Well, Mrs. Werner, let's give him some time. Maybe my being here will help."

The housekeeper nodded. "I surely hope so." She handed Anne a cloth-covered basket. "You'll be eating lunch with him, I expect. See what you can do about getting him to eat."

Anne smiled. "I'll do my best." She set the basket on the counter. "I think I'll have a better chance if I add the strudel." She carefully wrapped the pastry with a piece of paper left over from packing their basket. "So what are you going to do with your morning off, Mrs. Werner?"

"I intend to visit my sister-in-law down in the south part of the city."

"That's a long walk; I hope you'll be careful."

"Oh, me old legs couldn't stand walking that far. I'll take the streetcar."

Anne glanced up, her interest piqued. "Columbus has streetcars?"

"Aye, horse-drawn, they are. They run along High Street, from Dodridge to the north to well past Broad Street. The last stop is near City Park, right where I'll be getting off."

Anne smiled. "Well that's good to know." *Yes*, she thought, *that* is *good to know*.

"It's not fast, mind you, and it smells something awful if your seat's in the wrong spot, but it's certainly better than walking."

"Anne?" Uncle Daniel poked his head in. "Are you ready? Neither of us should be late on the first day." He smiled at Mrs. Werner. "Thank you for breakfast this morning."

Mrs. Werner opened her mouth to say something just as his head disappeared. "That man!"

Anne laughed. "I'll make him eat something at lunch, I promise."

Basket in hand, Anne walked to the front hall where her uncle waited for her. She eyed the hall clock. "I thought you said we were late."

"If we're to take a trip out to the stable first, we'll need extra time."

"I should have known," she said, taking his arm.

"I'd ask you if you mind, but I know better," Daniel said as they walked. "You didn't think your Pa wouldn't tell me the regard you have for my horse, now did you?"

"Of course not." Anne sighed. "He told you to keep me out of the stable, didn't he?"

He stopped and looked at her. "He told some other things as well. I'm very sorry, Anne."

She felt him squeeze her hand where it sat in the crook of his arm. "Pa's hoping I'll make a match down here and forget about what happened."

"Is that what you want?"

Yes nearly escaped her lips. "I don't know if I'll ever really forget."

"I can understand that. Pain can leave a lasting and bitter aftertaste." His eyes sobered then he smiled gently. "I know my brother. He wants what's best for you. And so does God. Trust them."

Anne tugged on his arm, trying to maintain a peaceful countenance. They walked on in silence for several moments.

"If you don't mind my asking," Uncle Daniel said, "all other matters aside, did you enjoy teaching?"

Anne smiled. When she decided to get a teaching certificate, her uncle had been delighted and given her every encouragement. Taking a breath, she tried to soften how she really felt as best she could. "I don't know. It wasn't awful. But I didn't enjoy it as much as I enjoyed working with our animals when I was younger. I can't remember liking anything better than that." She looked at him in wide-eyed apology. "I'm sorry."

He chuckled and patted her hand. "Don't be, but I can't imagine you'll enjoy the library much better."

"I know." Her uncle's house sat close to High Street and she caught a glimpse of a streetcar going past. Her true reason for taking the library job twisted her heart so much it was hard to form her next words. "But it's only for a few months."

"True, I had forgotten Miss Fuller hopes to return from her convalescence just before the spring term starts." He squeezed her hand again and she turned back to him. "You're always welcome to visit Scioto. I'll be praying for you."

When they reached the stable, Uncle Daniel opened the door for her and she immediately saw Scioto at his stall door. He grunted as they walked over to him. Daniel stroked his horse's neck, reminding Anne of how her uncle used to be before Aunt Kat died. She scratched the horse's withers, noticing he hadn't yet been groomed. She looked in Scioto's feed bin to see if he had finished eating. It certainly appeared he had; so why wasn't Ben brushing him down? She'd always groomed him just after he ate. She was about to say something to her uncle when the young stable hand appeared.

"Good morning, Professor Kirby, Miss Kirby," he said with a smile.

Anne nodded and her uncle quickly turned to him. "How has he been spending the night?"

"Very well, sir, I hardly ever hear him."

"Is he behaving better for you now?"

"Yes, sir, he's a little less fractious, now that we've gotten to know each other a little."

Uncle Daniel chuckled. "I'm afraid he's always been like that. With the exception of my niece here and... my late wife, he's never taken well to new people."

"I was just getting ready to let him out in the paddock a while."

"If you don't mind, I'll lead him out," Uncle Daniel said eagerly. He took the lead from Ben and snapped it onto Scioto's halter.

Anne laid her hand on Ben's arm before he could follow Scioto and her uncle. "Ben, I was wondering something about Scioto—"

"Don't worry, Miss Kirby," he said quickly. "I'll take real good care of him."

Remembering how Pa had told her to stay out of Ben's way, she nodded. "Of course you will."

She watched him join her uncle. She truly hoped Ben would take care of Scioto, considering how attached her uncle was to his horse. But Ben was young—seventeen—and a little too eager to please and prove himself. She shook her head. Scioto's daily care wasn't her responsibility any longer. People had different ways of doing things. Perhaps Ben didn't see the point in grooming him until after Scioto had been exercised. She hoped he would remember. Scioto trotted around the perimeter of the paddock before loping over to Uncle Daniel. He smiled and gave him a final pat.

"I'll be back, old boy." He shook Ben's hand then joined Anne. She watched his face lengthen a little, and she mustered a cheerful smile as she took his arm.

"We can come back this evening and spend more time with him," she suggested as they made their way back to the front of the house.

He shook his head. "We won't have time, I'm afraid. If you recall, Dr. Townshend invited us to his home tonight. He's sending a carriage for us." He glanced back at his horse. "I'd have Scioto take us but he's still getting used to it here, and I haven't gotten a new buggy yet."

"Then we'll visit him tomorrow morning."

He nodded slowly and Anne decided she would make sure Ben took proper care of her uncle's horse. Promise or no, she couldn't stand to think of the melancholy Uncle Daniel would sink into should something happen to Scioto.

Chapter 4

"I thought four o'clock would never get here!"

Anne smiled at Emma's exclamation as the young assistant librarian closed the door. It had been an exhausting first day. Never had she imagined that working at the library would be so similar to teaching, at least regarding discipline. She'd spent a great deal of the day attempting to keep the students quiet and the young men from propping their feet up on the windowsills and tables. At one point, when a young lady had fetched them to help get some reference material, several young men had situated their feet on the shelves such that it was impossible to access the tome she required. Some had actually removed books from the shelves and set them aside to make room for their feet. They hadn't bothered to replace them. Anne and Emma now took up the numerous volumes sitting about and began to reshelve them.

Anne looked around as they worked. She couldn't help but admire the library's new home on the third floor of the Main Building. She'd been told the room used to belong to the botanical department. They had moved upon the completion of their own building, opening up this space. It was a large room with elegant wooden columns running down the middle. The smell of fresh wood still hung in the air from the newly built shelves and broad tables for students to work at stood in neat rows. Anne sighed as she looked at all the books stacked on them now. The library seemed to have so many volumes already, and yet Emma had told her the university intended to acquire more!

She looked at the sunshine dancing in from one of the windows, longing to step outside. There hadn't been one opportunity to do so all day, not even at lunchtime since Uncle Daniel's office was just down the hall. When she had been teaching, she'd always made it a habit to step outside for at least a few minutes during the day.

Emma set down a stack of books at the sound of a knock at the door. "I'll bet that's that engineering student, begging to be let back in for just one more peek at a book." Her huff poofed up her brown fringe of curly bangs. "I'll shoo him back to his dormitory."

Anne chuckled as she took an armful of books to where they belonged. She heard Emma open the door, but judging from the tone of her voice, it must not have been him. The door closed and a moment or two later when she returned to the study tables for more books, Emma was there.

"Mike Dixon, the university janitor, sent his assistant over to check the gas pipes before cold weather sets in," she said, taking up a stack of books. "He won't be but a few minutes."

Anne nodded and took up a particularly large book. She walked over to its shelf only to find that she was too short to put it back where it belonged. She grimaced in disgust, wishing yet again she were a respectable height. "Emma, do we have a step stool?"

"It's back in the corner, near the science shelf. Sorry it's tucked away, but I hardly ever use it."

Anne sighed. Of course Emma didn't use it. She was at least four inches taller than Anne. She walked over to the corner and spied the stool. She was so intent on fetching it and getting back to work, she didn't notice the janitor's assistant working close by. She knelt down and grasped it, barely moving it an inch before she shrieked. A spider scurried out and sat on the wooden floor, all too close to the hem of her skirt. Anne froze in fear. The vile thing was the size of a large walnut and just as black. The sound of her name being called began to register in her mind as a brown boot came out of nowhere, crushing the spider. She gasped and looked up into a pair of emerald eyes. Their owner offered his hand. "Are you all right?"

She reached out a shaky hand and felt his fingers fold over her own. Somehow their warmth helped steady her racing heart as he helped her to her feet. Emma popped out from between the shelves and hurried over. "Anne, are you all right? What happened?"

"A spider gave her a fright." The quiet manner in which the man said it gratified Anne. Most thought her fear of spiders silly. He lifted his boot and gently squeezed her hand as she looked away in revulsion. Emma's face registered disgust as well and she shuddered.

"I'll clean this up, Miss Long," he said, handing Anne off to Emma.

She found herself releasing his hand reluctantly and couldn't help but look back at him as Emma gently grasped her by the elbow. His voice sounded young, but his full beard and mustache made her wonder if he was much older. He knelt down, took out a handkerchief, and wiped up the remains of the spider. "Thank you," she said, hoping to catch sight of his green eyes once more. But they remained focused on his task and he simply nodded.

Peter's heart raced. She wouldn't have been hurt, of course; wolf spiders weren't poisonous, but the sight of them was anything but pleasant. What set his heart at such a pace was his first sight of Anne Kirby.

He'd known when he'd taken the job working for Mr. Dixon he might cross paths with Professor Kirby's niece. He just hadn't expected it to happen so soon or in such a way. Normally, he would have caught the spider and let it go, but the look of fright on her face compelled him to crush the thing.

And he certainly hadn't expected her to be even more beautiful in person. Her small build, porcelain skin, and ginger-red hair made her look just like one of the china dolls he'd seen in the shops back in Pittsburgh.

Stop it, he told himself sharply. She wasn't a toy for him to play with, but a person. He tried to reinforce that thought in his mind by remembering the fear in her brown doe eyes, and how shaky her hand had been as he helped her to her feet. Peter shook his head. Thinking of her like that didn't help either.

He wadded up his handkerchief and, not seeing a trash can handy, placed it in his pocket. He'd shake it out and wash it later. He finished his work, placed the tools Mr. Dixon had given him in their bag, and slipped out the door. He struggled to push thoughts of Miss Kirby from his mind as he made his way over the gravel walkway to the new botany building.

Setting his jaw, he tried to go over the list of things Mr. Dixon wanted him to check, but all he heard was her soft voice, thanking him, making it hard to concentrate. Why had he helped her to her feet? He still felt the gentle pressure of her fingers on his. Peter was so focused on his thoughts he bumped into someone as he walked.

"Hey, watch where you're going!"

"Sorry," he said. He began to move on when someone grabbed his arm. Frowning, Peter turned to see a dark-haired man a few years older than him. Another man stood beside him, thumbs in his suspenders.

"Who are you? What do you think you're doing with that bag?"

His superior tone sparked Peter's temper but he managed to answer civilly. "I'm Peter Ward, the janitor's assistant. Mr. Dixon gave me this bag this morning."

"No, I know all the fellas Mike uses as assistants," he said. "I've never seen you before."

Peter noticed the man with the suspenders looked at

him with a glimmer of recognition in his eyes and was instantly on his guard. Had he been sent by his uncle? He quickly decided to be on his way.

"Well, I'm new. Now if you two gentlemen will excuse me—"

The first man grabbed his arm. "Whoa! How about this guy? Us 'two gentlemen'? Pretty fancy talk for a janitor."

Suspenders gave him a hard look. "Mike said he was going to hire me for fall term. Why'd he hire you, fancypants?"

Peter narrowed his eyes, sorely tempted to give them the fight they sought but held back. He needed this job and the anonymity it provided. Gently, but firmly, he freed his arm. "I have to go. Mr. Dixon has things for me to do."

Scowls crossed their faces and Peter steeled himself for a fight just as Mike Dixon walked up.

"There you are, Pete. I've been looking for you." He caught sight of the men. "Hello there, Frank. What are you and Harvey up to?"

"I brought Harvey by like you said." Frank pointed to the man with the suspenders.

"What's with this guy?" Harvey jabbed his finger toward Peter.

Peter worked his jaw but kept his mouth shut.

Mike sighed and stepped up to him. "I'm sorry, Harvey. Pete really needed a job. He's been out of work for a while."

"Then why doesn't Mr. Cope know about him? We just saw him a few minutes ago, and he didn't think you'd hired anyone yet."

"He will. I'm going to tell the board at their next meeting."

"You never did that before," Frank said. "You always told them before you hired anyone."

"There wasn't time. This came up at the last minute." Peter looked at him. Mike sounded like he'd hired him only yesterday. He'd been working a couple of weeks now.

Harvey glared at him. "I need a job, Mike."

"I'm sorry, but I don't have the funds for you."

"Yes you do," Frank said. "The university always gives you enough for two extra men fall term."

"Well not this year."

Frank frowned and shook his head at Harvey. His face scrunched up like that of a sulky schoolboy and Peter choked back a laugh. "You just don't want to hire me do you?"

"To be honest, I can't say I've ever heard good things about you," Mike said. "I'm sorry."

Both men glared at Mike for one long, tense moment. Peter hoped it wouldn't come to blows but was ready to help if his boss needed him.

"Fine." Harvey said finally. "Let's go, Frank." The two veered off the gravel path, stomping through the newly cut grass.

Mike shook his head. "Jack will need to rake that now," he said, referring to the groundskeeper.

"Who's Mr. Cope?" Peter asked.

"The secretary to the board of trustees," he replied. "Don't worry. I've worked here since '78. I'm sure they won't mind me hiring someone without their approval. They've never refused anyone before, even someone like Harvey Pryce." He pointed his thumb in the direction the men had gone. "Come on, let's finish up in the Botany Building and get dinner."

An hour or so later, Peter and Mike sat down to eat in Mike's log cabin, which stood on university grounds. It had been there since before the university's founding and when the state bought up the land, the cabin had been deeded over to the institution. Mike said it hadn't been used until the university offered it to him just a few years ago. He'd installed a potbellied stove, which Peter now stood over, frying up some ham for them both.

"You sure took to the cooking real quick," Mike said as Peter slid meat onto his plate. "It's kind of hard to believe you'd never done it before."

"Well, not over a stove. I learned to cook a lot of things over an open fire." Peter put another slab of ham in the cast-iron skillet.

"So you really were a tramp, huh?"

"Not by choice," he replied with a half-smile.

"If you don't mind me asking, just where are you originally from?"

Peter looked at his boss a moment before answering, then laughed at himself for hesitating. Mike Dixon, a kind and simple man, was by no means stupid but hardly a Pinkerton agent working undercover. "Pittsburgh."

Mike nodded. "Never been there, heard about it though. Those steel mills sure put out a lot of smoke I hear."

Peter bent to tend to the fire in the stove, hiding a small smile as he did so. "Yeah, they sure do."

He carried the skillet to the table and slid his meat onto his plate then returned it to the stove. He sat down next to Mike. The older man worded a small prayer before they started on their meal.

"Did you get to the pipes in Main Building?" Mike asked as they ate.

"Yes I did, Mr. Dixon."

The man rolled his eyes. "Son, do me a favor. *Please* call me Mike. Even the students call me that."

Peter smiled. "All right."

It would be odd, though. Mr. Dixon—Mike—was several years older than he. Granddad may have given him free rein in most areas, but he'd insisted Peter respect his elders.

"Everything in Main Building seemed fine," he said.

"You checked the new library, too?" Peter nodded, and Mike smiled in approval. "Good. It won't do for students to catch cold while they're studying, not to mention those young ladies who work so hard keeping that place looking nice." He shot Peter a grin. "Did you get a chance to meet them? They're just about your age."

"Ah—yes. Miss Long introduced herself. I didn't get the other young lady's name." It was true. He'd been too busy cleaning up that spider.

"She's Professor Kirby's niece, I hear. They're pretty girls, too."

Peter smiled at the look the man gave him. "I've got too much to do right now to think about things like that."

Mike's eyebrows shot up. "Well that's a surprise. But I suppose I understand. Never did decide to get married myself. A lot of fuss, women. Not that I don't appreciate them. Just seems easier to be on your own, you know?"

"Yeah," Peter said thoughtfully. All those days of chasing Pittsburgh's eligible young ladies came back to him. He'd never been serious about any of them. For one reason or another, none of them seemed right—too tall, too short, too something. Or had that been just an excuse? He pushed the ham around on his plate with his fork. Not all of them had been like that. He could have fallen in love with at least one or two, if he'd allowed himself. Well, those days were over now. He'd told the truth a moment ago. He was too busy to be thinking about courting someone. He didn't intend to ever try again. But even as he made that vow, doe-like eyes and a sweet face filled his vision.

He sighed inwardly as he picked up his plate and took it over to the washtub. The whole reason he'd turned down the job with Professor Kirby was so he wouldn't be tempted to return to his old habits. And he would have, if he'd stayed. Look at the way he had behaved today, acting like some sort of knight-errant. He shouldn't have allowed the professor to help him get this job with Mike, but after seeing how his refusal to work for him had disappointed the man, he hadn't had the heart. Well, at least Anne Kirby worked in the library. The chances of him seeing her again were quite slim.

Peter helped Mike clean up the dinner plates, and then settled down at the table with his Bible while his boss sat and whittled. Dr. Kirby had insisted Peter keep it when he left. At the time he'd felt bad that he couldn't pay him for the book, but at the moment he was glad. With Anne Kirby's beauty running rampant in his head, he flipped back and forth through its pages, looking for a verse on self-control. As he still wasn't familiar with it, he quickly came up empty.

Frustrated, he stopped. The pages fell open to the book of Psalms. As he idly skimmed them, the twenty-third caught his attention:

The Lord is my shepherd; I shall not want. He maketh me to lie down in green pastures: he leadeth me beside the still waters. He restoreth my soul: he leadeth me in the paths of righteousness for his name's sake.

He sat back, staring out the cabin's narrow window. It was a heartening verse and gave him hope. The idea of the Lord leading him in his new life, looking out for pitfalls along the way, made him feel more at ease. *Lord, lead me in the right path; show me where You want me to go,* he prayed. *I know with Your guidance I can throw away my past and begin again.* He was a new creation now, and that meant he should desire a whole new life, one without horses or chasing young ladies.

Chapter 5

Anne entered her room with a frown creasing her lovely features. When she and Uncle Daniel returned to the house, he'd urged her to get ready quickly, as Dr. Townshend's carriage was coming for them in less than an hour. But she hadn't been able to resist slipping out to the barn to check on Scioto. To her consternation, while the horse seemed content enough, he was wild and shaggy looking, as if he hadn't been near a brush and currycomb all day. And Ben was nowhere to be found.

Though not nearly as thorough as she would have liked, she quickly brushed him. What could Ben have been thinking? Scioto wasn't a plow horse. Uncle Daniel intended to ride him every so often and use him to convey the two of them back and forth to church. He may be an older horse, but he was still a strong animal. Professor Townshend had even brought a couple of his mares up to the farm this summer to breed with him. Anne opened the door of her room and found Mrs. Werner waiting for her.

"There you are," she exclaimed. "Dr. Kirby fetched me almost fifteen minutes ago to help you get dressed." The housekeeper frowned and crinkled her nose. "You went out in the stable, didn't you?"

"Oh no! I smell like horse, don't I?" She unbuttoned her bodice. "Maybe it's just my clothes."

Happily that was the case, and soon she stood in front of her oval mirror in her best dress. It was dark green with three-quarter sleeves. Anne smiled, remembering Pa's frown when she, Ma, and Millie had shown it to him. He hadn't quite approved of the square neckline. But Ma had been careful to make sure it was more than proper. It was actually shallower than the one on the dress she and Millie had copied from *Godey's Lady's Book*. Tears pricked her eyes as she thought how hard they'd worked, making this just for her to wear for best. She fingered the ruffles at the end of her sleeve and resolved to take special care of it. It would be a reminder of them once she was far from Ohio. Mrs. Werner began to fuss with her hair, and Anne glanced at the clock on her bed table.

"I'm not sure there's time, Mrs. Werner."

"Now, now, I'm just going to re-pin a few of these ringlets. You fluff those curly bangs of yours."

Anne did as she was told just as her uncle's voice came from behind her door. "Anne, are you ready? Dr. Townshend's carriage is here."

She escaped from the housekeeper's hands and rushed to the wardrobe to get her shoes. A small spider scrambled out as she did so, and she gasped then crushed it with one shoe.

"What is it, lass?" Mrs. Werner joined her by the wardrobe.

Anne stood with one hand across her chest, trying to still the quick leaps her heart was making. "Just a spider," she murmured.

"A spider?" Mrs. Werner smiled. "I thought you'd seen worse than that."

Anne's face reddened slightly as she slipped on her shoes. Her fear of spiders was so silly. She'd grown up on a farm, for heaven's sake. But she couldn't remember a time when she hadn't been afraid of them. A small one like that didn't affect her badly, but if it were a large one like the wolf spider she encountered in the library, fear refused to allow her to move an inch. She shuddered to think where that spider might have crawled if the janitor's assistant hadn't killed it. Her heart quickened once more as she thought of the man's green eyes and the gentle firmness of his fingers squeezing hers. He'd been so kind and gallant. *Stop that. None of that for you, remember?*

"Anne?" Her uncle's voice came from the bottom of the stairs this time, and she quickly took her wrap and reticule from Mrs. Werner. She had every intention of explaining why she was late as her uncle hurried her out the door, when she saw a young man she didn't recognize sitting in the carriage. She'd have to wait to talk to her uncle about Ben.

"Good evening, Patrick," Uncle Daniel said as he helped Anne climb up. "I'm sorry we're a little late."

Anne settled into the rear seat and took in the young

man who sat opposite her. He was handsome with blond hair and a mustache, and he wore a sack suit and bowler hat. Uncle Daniel settled in next to her. She looked at him expectantly.

"Ah yes, I forgot you two aren't yet acquainted," he said as the carriage lurched forward. "Mr. Howard, this is my niece, Miss Anne Kirby. Anne, Mr. Patrick Howard, one of Dr. Townsend's students."

"I'm pleased to meet you, Mr. Howard."

He tipped his hat and shot her a charming smile. "The pleasure is mine, Miss Kirby. I hope you'll enjoy yourself tonight. The rest of us are looking forward to meeting you."

Curious, Anne glanced at her uncle.

"Oh yes," he said. "I forgot to mention there would be a few upperclassmen there as well." His eyebrows rose along with the right corner of his mouth.

Anne bit the inside of her lip. Uncle Daniel had led her to believe the other dinner guests were limited to the faculty and their wives. Clearly, Pa had gotten him to promise more than just limiting her time in the stable. Her eyes slid back to Mr. Howard, and taking a deep breath, she smiled politely. "Are you a farmer, Mr. Howard?"

"My family owns a dairy farm near Lodi. I hope to become a veterinary surgeon."

"Mr. Howard is a senior this year, Anne," her uncle said. "He'll be graduating at the top of his class."

"Well, I hope to," the young man replied humbly. "I understand your family lives in Ostrander, Miss Kirby."

The three of them chatted the rest of the way to Professor Townshend's home at the edge of the university's grounds. As they pulled up, Anne looked at the cozy home with no small amount of trepidation. The evening would be difficult for her if the rest of the young men at the party were as nice as Patrick Howard. She thought coming to the university to work would be easier than this. She had only been here a week and she seemed to be surrounded by eligible men. If only she were an eligible young woman. As Mr. Howard helped her alight, he held the same hand the janitor's assistant had grasped. The memory of his green eyes and gallant actions caused her to sigh.

"Are you all right, Miss Kirby?" Mr. Howard asked.

"Yes of course." She accepted the arm he offered.

At least there, she was safe. She couldn't possibly see much of him in the future. Besides, he had to be much older than her, and married with about a dozen children. She couldn't help but envy his wife. If he was half so gallant at home, she was a blessed woman.

It was an animated dinner. There were Dr. and Mrs. Townshend and their two daughters, Alice and Harriet; Professors Lazenby, Tuttle, and Orton, and their wives; and five male students, including Mr. Howard. It came as no small surprise when she found herself surrounded by them after dinner when the party retired to the parlor after they ate.

"So what do you think of The O.S.U.?" one of them asked her. He had been introduced as George Smart, a philosophy major and editor-in-chief of *The Lantern,* the university paper.

"*The* O.S.U.?" she asked with a smile.

"Surely your uncle told you we are *The* Ohio State University."

"Yes, but I'm not sure why."

"The board of trustees decided that our original name, the Ohio Agricultural and Mechanical College, wasn't a broad enough name for our institution. After all, more is taught here than agriculture and mechanical engineering. Calling us 'The Ohio State University' fulfills that idea and sets us apart from the other colleges in Ohio."

"Be careful, Mr. Smart. Pride goeth before destruction…" Anne warned.

"You think there's something wrong in being proud of one's university, Miss Kirby?" another young man asked. Anne couldn't quite remember his name but recalled he was an arts major.

"No, but it doesn't seem very Christian to look down on the other fine institutions Ohio has to offer," she replied.

"You misunderstand me, Miss Kirby." Mr. Smart smiled. "None of us look down on any of the other colleges here in Ohio or anywhere else." The other students murmured in assent. "We just want The O.S.U. to be one of the best educational institutions in the country. Mark my words, one day we will be."

"I've heard the library is certainly getting us off on the right foot," Mr. Howard said. "I understand the new location in the Main Building is much larger."

"I didn't have the opportunity to see the library in the old room, but the new one is quite impressive," Anne replied.

"I'm sure your presence and hard work make it even

more so." Mr. Howard smiled broadly. "I'll have to visit sometime very soon."

"Yes, Pat, with the start of the new term, I'm sure we'll all make time to visit—and often," George added.

The men nodded, and it wasn't lost on Anne that their library visits would be more than just educational in nature. She politely returned their smiles, all the while clenching her teeth, determined to politely rebuff them when the time came. She hated to have to do it. They were all very nice young men, but she wasn't what they were looking for in a wife.

Anne excused herself and joined her uncle, who was talking with Professor Townshend. "I'm glad those two mares seem to be working out," he said as she approached.

"Yes, they should foal next summer," Dr. Townshend replied. He smiled broadly at her approach. "Well, Anne, how nice to see you."

"Hello, Dr. Townshend." The professor had been with the university since its inception and a great help to her brother when he had been one of its first agricultural students.

"How is your brother?" he asked.

"Jacob is doing very well. He speaks of you often."

"I'm glad he and your father were able to attend the free lecture we gave last year."

"They went on about it for days after they returned," Anne replied. "If you'll excuse me, but were you and my uncle talking about the two mares you brought to the farm to breed with Scioto a few months ago?"

"Yes, we were," Uncle Daniel replied. He gave her

a warning look, but she ignored it in her enthusiasm to find out about the mares' condition.

"I would love to see them foal when the time comes," she said eagerly.

"Really?" Anne turned to see Patrick Howard standing behind her, his eyebrows raised. "That can be a rather distressing sight, Miss Kirby."

Seeing a way of getting rid of at least one potential suitor, she went on. "I don't think I'd find it distressing in the least, Mr. Howard."

"Oh, you don't?"

Relief shot through her as the puzzled look on the young man's face told her she had hit her mark. But it evaporated when her uncle looked reprovingly at her. Dr. Townshend quickly changed the subject and began to discuss the hopes he and Professor Lazenby had for the relatively new Agricultural Experiment Station.

Later, it wasn't surprising when Patrick Howard excused himself from accompanying them on their short trip home. Her uncle remained quiet as they rode, and Anne didn't pretend to not know why. She had no desire to talk about it. But the silence was stifling. Eventually she spoke just to clear it.

"I wonder if it will rain tonight," she said.

"You didn't ruin your chances with just him, you know." It was hard to see his expression in the dark, but his quiet tone painted a clear picture. "Those other four young men room in the same boardinghouse."

"I'm…I'm sorry, Uncle Daniel. It's just—" Tears edged her voice. She regretted what she had done, but what else could she do?

Her uncle misread her sadness and took her hand.

"I'm sorry, Anne. I ambushed you tonight. But your ma and pa and I, we want to see you settled. You must at least try."

Anne dabbed at her eyes and turned the conversation around. She didn't want to make a promise she couldn't keep. "What about you, Uncle Daniel?"

"What about me?"

"You've been sad, too. Mrs. Werner told me about Mr. Ward." He still held her hand, and she squeezed it. "I'm sorry, I know you miss Joseph."

For several minutes, he said nothing, and only the crunch and hiss of the gravel under the carriage wheels and the clop of the horse's feet echoed in the background.

"I had hoped he would stay," Uncle Daniel said finally, his voice soft and distant. "It seemed like he wanted to. I don't understand why he didn't. It was like having him back again."

Anne felt tears beginning to reassert themselves and quickly swallowed them. "But Joseph will be back for Christmas, won't he? And Rebecca will be here with her husband?"

"What? Oh yes, I got a letter from each of them a few days ago. They'll be home for Christmas."

"There then, you'll have them both back for a few days at least. That's something we can both take comfort in and look forward to."

Her uncle nodded. "Yes, you're right. I guess it was a little foolish of me to pine away for the past." He sounded a little more like himself. "We both must be about 'forgetting those things which are behind, and reaching forth unto those things which are before.' "

She swallowed, her smile fading. "I'll try."

"As for me, having Scioto here now is a blessing and a comfort."

The house and stable came into view. She didn't like having to tell him about Ben now, but in light of what he just said, he needed to know. "I'm sorry I was late coming down. But I just had to slip out to see Scioto before I got dressed."

Her uncle listened quietly as she told him about his horse's condition, how she'd quickly brushed him down, and her concerns about Ben. By the time she finished, they stood on the front porch. From the light of the oil lamp shining through the parlor window, she could make out his stern expression.

"I promised your pa I would keep you from doing anything more than visiting Scioto," he said quietly. "You promised him the same. How do you know Ben wasn't out fetching something he needed? He could also have been out having his dinner."

Anne lowered her gaze. Neither of those things had occurred to her. "I'm sorry, Uncle Daniel."

"Let Ben take care of Scioto," he said gently.

October 1884

Peter walked toward the lecture room where chapel was held. The short faculty-led devotional took place every day in the Main Building at this time and was mandatory for every student. Ever since Mike had given him the task of sweeping up the room afterward, he managed to time the rest of his duties so he would arrive to catch all if not most of the service. He stood outside the door, of course. Although no one had ever discouraged him from doing so, he didn't feel right sitting in on the services.

He could hear the student choir singing as he approached, indicating that they had only just started. Taking his usual spot next to the room's double doors, he leaned himself and his broom against the wall, wondering which of the faculty would speak today. Whoever it was, he hoped they would read a passage from scripture. Many times one of the professors simply read from the writings of a renowned theologian, and once, a passage from Emerson had been read. But when a passage of the Bible was chosen, the comments afterward were always enlightening. There were still portions of the Bible that left Peter completely lost, and this was the only opportunity he had to have scripture explained to him. Mike kept close to the university on Sundays, and the day usually entailed them singing a hymn or two and reading from one of the gospels.

The choir began another song, and Peter's mind wandered to the other tasks Mike had assigned to him today. His boss was very pleased with how well he had taken to his job. Peter seemed to have a knack for fixing things. It would appear that God had answered his prayers about His path for his life. *Then why aren't I happy about it?* He found himself still yearning to be around horses. A great number of his duties were around or near the university farm buildings. Every time he saw the horses stabled there, he felt a pang of longing and envied the students assigned to care for them.

Then there was Anne Kirby. Try as he might—

"Please let me know if you find any more spiders. My boot is at your service."

The professor looked at Anne with raised eyebrows. "I encountered a spider my first day at the library, Uncle Daniel," she said. "Mr. Ward was kind enough to kill it for me." His heart swelled at the little smile she bestowed on him. "Thank you, again."

"Not at all," he replied. Their eyes locked for a moment, and he swore he saw something other than melancholy color in them, but it quickly vanished. He carefully closed the Bible on the podium and handed it to her.

"If I'm not mistaken, this goes with you." Their fingers brushed, and he thought he could power the whole university with the surge that the brief contact triggered. He thrust his hands in his pockets.

"If you will excuse me," Anne said. "I really should get back to the library."

"Of course," Dr. Kirby said. A gentle sort of sternness colored his voice. "We'll talk later."

She nodded, and with a final glance at Peter, left the room. He didn't realize he was still looking at the door until the professor grasped his shoulder. Words of apology sat on his tongue, but he didn't need them.

"Thank you," the professor said.

"Sir?"

"That's the first smile I've seen from her in a week. I guess you can surmise what happened to her from what you overheard."

Peter nodded. "I'll pray for her, sir." He almost regretted making that promise, but he didn't like the weariness that suddenly lined the professor's face. God would just have to help him handle whatever feelings praying for Anne evoked. He rubbed the back of his neck. "But I am sorry that I overheard your conversation. I had no idea you both were standing there."

"Don't be. Probably best that you know how shamefully she was treated, so you can be clear in your prayers." The professor pulled out his pocket watch then snapped it shut. "I should go. My next class is waiting for me." He shook Peter's hand and left.

Peter retrieved his broom from the hall, and as he swept the lecture hall, he wished he could sweep away his guilt as easily. He'd never seen the other side of his actions before, never seen the condition of the hearts he'd left broken. Seeing the sadness in Miss Kirby's eyes gave him an excruciatingly clear picture. *Lord, please allow her heart to be healed of its hurts. And forgive me for ever doing to anyone what was done to her.* The words of the Psalm returned to his mind. *Restore her soul.*

Chapter 6

Anne climbed the stairs to the library with shaky steps. She hadn't imagined that the janitor's assistant was the same young man her uncle had helped over a month ago. Since that was clearly the case, then he certainly wasn't married. It had been easier to keep thoughts of him far from her mind when she'd imagined him with a wife and children. She stopped on the landing between the second and third floors. *It will still be easy, once you go into town tomorrow.* Tomorrow was Saturday, and her uncle had a faculty meeting for a large portion of the day. If she could get by Mrs. Werner, she intended to take the streetcar into the city. She couldn't wait any longer. The prospect made her feet turn to water as she continued.

"There you are," Emma said as Anne walked back into the library. She took the Bible from her. "Are you all right?"

"Fine," Anne replied. "Those stairs can be quite a chore."

"Yes, it's taking me some time getting used to running up and down them myself."

Anne looked around the library. Shelves blocked some of her view of the room, but from what she could see and hear, it seemed empty. "I guess we better shelve some books while we have the chance." A mysterious smile formed on Emma's lips. "What?"

"Nothing," she said a little too brightly. She took the Bible from Anne. "I'll start with this. I think there are some books lying on a shelf on the far side of the room."

Anne walked between two shelves to the open area where the study tables sat. Patrick Howard sat at one of them with a mythology book lying open before him. She knew studying was not his motivation for his visit. She sighed. This was the third time in as many weeks that he'd come to the library specifically to visit her. What she had said at Dr. Townshend's party hadn't deterred him for long. He'd clearly seen the advantage in the possibility of a wife who had no trouble seeing animals born.

She stepped back and leaned against the shelf. With the exception of Mr. Howard, she may have put off the other young men from the party, but there were certainly more where they came from. Several eligible young men had approached her since the term started. With few exceptions, the majority of them were nice, and Anne truly hated discouraging them. Each time she did so, it was a reminder that her chance to become someone's wife and helpmeet was no longer possible, the reason she'd become sad and moody over the past month. She peeked out at where Mr. Howard sat. She might as well get this one over with.

She stepped out from between the shelves, and he looked up and smiled at her.

"Good afternoon, Miss Kirby."

Anne pasted on a polite smile. "How are you today, Mr. Howard?"

"Very fine, thank you. I enjoyed your uncle's reading during chapel. It's nice hearing the 23rd Psalm recited with such meaning. It was as if he were trying to give someone a bit of comfort."

Anne's smile flattened a little. "Is *Bullfinch's Mythology* required reading now for a degree in agriculture?"

Mr. Howard's face reddened. "No, it was just sitting here when I came in." He stood and walked over to her. "The weather has been very fine, lately, and I wanted to ask if you would be interested in accompanying me and some other students to Goodale Park tomorrow. I understand from your uncle you have no plans."

His invitation caused Anne to pause. Goodale Park, according to her uncle, was close to the city. Accepting might be to her advantage.

"Oh but I'm not a student, Mr. Howard. Would the others want me along?" If she accepted too quickly, he and Uncle Daniel—who was clearly in on this—might suspect something.

"It's all upperclassmen, Miss Kirby. Seniors, mostly." Hope shone in his eyes. "Please come, we'd love to have you."

"Very well, Mr. Howard, you can count me in."

If Mr. Howard was pleased with her response, her uncle was even more so when she told him as they walked home that evening.

"I'm glad, Anne. Patrick Howard is a fine young man." He smiled down at her. "I guess that Psalm helped more than either of us thought."

Anne looked away as she remembered listening to the 23rd Psalm in chapel that day. She knew Uncle Daniel had meant well, but she wished he hadn't read it. Hearing what had once been such a source of comfort for her was now almost akin to torture. The words *"He restoreth my soul"* echoed mockingly in her ears. How was that possible now? Tears toyed with the edges of her vision. She stumbled a little and firmly grasped her uncle's arm. He, in turn, slowed to steady her. "Careful now, it won't do for you to twist your ankle."

"No, it won't." She looked out over the darkening university grounds. "Will you have a chance to visit Scioto when we get home?"

Her uncle paused for a moment then sighed heavily. "No, I'm afraid, not again tonight. Too many papers to grade." He hefted the leather satchel. "You know, when I told you a month ago to let Ben take care of him, I never meant that you should stop visiting him altogether. He misses you."

"Does he?"

"Of course, horses are social by nature. He's wondering where the main member of his herd has gone."

She could just make out his wink in the dusk and had to chuckle. "Uncle Daniel, are you trying to tell me I resemble a horse?"

Her uncle laughed. "Hardly, but I really should see

about getting a stable mate for him. Since you seem less interested in visiting him—"

"It's not that I don't want to see him," she said softly. Nothing could be further from the truth. "I'm just trying to stay out of trouble."

In her mind, her departure approached far too quickly. Only yesterday Emma had mentioned that Clara Fuller, the young woman Anne was filling in for, was doing well and might return as early as the first of the year. Anne had realized it would probably be easier on both her and Scioto if she visited infrequently. After her uncle rebuked her for brushing him down, she'd gone to see him a few times, but over the past couple of weeks, she hadn't been out to the stable at all.

"Ben's doing fine with him," Uncle Daniel said. Anne hoped that was true. Now that the term was in full swing, her uncle rarely had time to go see him, and when he did, it was in the evening. It was hard to tell just how well a horse looked in lamplight. "You'll see for yourself tomorrow. I intend to ride him over to the faculty meeting."

The next morning, something about Scioto didn't seem quite right when her uncle led him out of the stable. Was it that his coat wasn't gleaming as brightly as she remembered? Or that he seemed to hold his head slightly lower than he had when she cared for him at home? Mr. Howard, who had arrived for their outing, seemed not to notice anything amiss.

"He's a fine animal, Dr. Kirby," he said. "He looks good for his age, too. A Morgan, isn't he?"

"Yes," Uncle Daniel replied. "I found him during

the war, after my own horse was shot out from under me. A year or two after the war ended, I was able to find out who he originally belonged to and pay them. He was quite valuable. You should see his bloodline."

"No wonder Dr. Townshend was eager to breed him. He is sure to be pleased when those foals come this summer," Mr. Howard replied.

Anne watched her uncle mount, still not quite satisfied by the way Scioto looked. Her uncle smiled, and prodding his horse into a slow trot, guided him down the path that led to the main road. She bit her lip. He seemed to be moving well enough. Maybe she was imagining things. She turned to find Ben leaning against the stable door.

"Is he eating well?" she asked.

Mr. Howard interrupted before the young man could answer. "Miss Kirby, of course he is. I would think even you could see that."

She arched an eyebrow at him. "Even me?"

"Not to be mean, but you're a librarian."

"But I was raised on a farm. I can tell when a horse looks ill."

"But *I* will eventually be a veterinarian. And I can tell you for certain that horse is as healthy as a horse his age can be." He pulled out his watch and glanced at it. "Are you ready? We really should be going. The streetcar will be coming by soon."

Anne looked in the direction her uncle had ridden. She didn't appreciate Mr. Howard's condescending attitude, but she had to admit he might be right. After all, she hadn't been out to see Scioto for quite a while.

"Yes, let's go." She took his arm. As they walked

down to the main road, Mr. Howard squinted against the morning sun toward High Street, the road that led directly into the city of Columbus.

"Come on," he said and began to walk faster. "The rest of our party is already at the streetcar stop, and I think I see it coming. We'll have to be quick to catch it."

It wasn't far, but Mr. Howard walked faster than Anne was used to and she stumbled.

"Oooh!" She stopped, and letting go of his arm, knelt down to grasp her ankle.

"Miss Kirby, are you all right? I'm so sorry!"

"I'll be fine, but I don't think I'll be able to come with you today." She rose and tried to put her weight on it then winced. "Ooh! No, I'm sorry."

"Then I won't go either."

"No, Mr. Howard, please don't give up your day on my account." She grabbed his arm. "Why don't you take me back to my house? It's only a few steps, and I'll get Mrs. Werner to come to the door. She'll look after me."

It took a little convincing, but she managed to get him to leave her at the front door. He waved as he ran to catch the streetcar and, as soon as he and the others were on it, Anne quietly opened the door. Once inside she peered down the front hall. She didn't see Mrs. Werner. The faint sound of an Irish tune being sung reached her ears. The housekeeper was busy in the kitchen, it seemed. Anne quietly made her way upstairs, her foot perfectly sound, and returned with a dark cloak and an old bonnet of her mother's. Bonnets were out of fashion, but it was the only way she knew to hide her face. Better to be out of fashion than be recognized. It would also make her seem a bit older.

She quietly let herself out and looked toward the street. Taking a deep breath, she walked down to High Street. Her heart pounding, she stepped onto the next car that stopped and settled herself down for the ride into Columbus.

Chapter 7

A yell and the throaty whinny of a horse caused Peter to stop his work and walk to the other side of Professor Tuttle's residence. Next door, outside Professor Kirby's stable, stood a bay horse, shaking his head and prancing. Dr. Kirby sat on the ground holding his arm, and Dr. Townshend knelt beside him. Peter immediately noticed the way the horse moved, favoring his front right hoof. Instinct took over and Peter jogged closer, slowing as he drew near.

"Are you all right, Professor Kirby?" he asked in a low voice.

"I'm fine. Peter, you'd best stay back. He can be fractious with people he doesn't know well."

But Peter slowly and calmly walked toward the horse. Speaking soothing words, he scratched him on his withers before reaching out and taking the reins. The horse calmed, although he bobbed his head and angled it several times toward his right hoof. Peter looked around. Didn't the professor have a stable hand? "Where is your man, sir?"

Both professors were staring at him. "I'm not sure where Ben is," Professor Kirby said slowly. "But you certainly have a way with him. He doesn't take to strangers well. Does he, Norton?"

Dr. Townshend shook his head. "It took a full week for him to get used to me the short time I was around him this past summer."

Peter looked away as he realized what he had just done. When he'd turned down Dr. Kirby's offer a month ago, he'd allowed the professor to believe it was because he knew next to nothing about horses, which certainly wasn't the case. Henry Farley was one of the best trainers in the business, and he'd agreed to leave a good-paying job in Philadelphia to work for Peter on one condition: that Peter learn to care for the horses he intended to own and race. As a result, he could handle any horse in any situation. Henry said he had "the touch." But it was a talent that he'd thought best to abandon, considering what it had cost him. Scioto shook his head again, and he automatically laid a steadying hand on his nose.

Dr. Kirby nodded toward them. "I'll be fine, Norton. Go help Peter."

The agriculture professor walked over and arched a questioning eyebrow at him. Peter avoided his eye, and Dr. Townshend ran his hands along Scioto's shoulder and down his leg, coaxing the animal to raise his foot. It didn't take much effort. Peter's brow furrowed as he caught a look at the back of the horse's lower leg. It was quite swollen.

"A sprained tendon," he blurted.

Professor Townshend looked at him and then at Dr. Kirby.

"He's right. He sprained a tendon, Daniel."

Dr. Kirby's face darkened. "I shouldn't have ridden him so hard. No wonder he threw me."

"I have a poultice that should help." Dr. Townshend gently lowered the foot as he described the treatment.

Peter nodded. It was the same one Henry had always used, and he knew it would produce good results. Dr. Kirby struggled to rise, and Peter handed Scioto off to Dr. Townshend to help him to his feet. Holding his injured arm to his chest, he slowly walked up to his horse.

"I'm sorry, old boy." He rubbed his neck with his good hand.

Peter spoke without thinking. "Don't worry sir, I know that poultice. It will work." Once again they both stared at him. "I—used to work in a barn. Once."

Dr. Townshend's eyebrows arched. "Young man, if I didn't already have more than enough students working at the university farm, I'd hire you on the spot."

"You know quite a bit for someone who has simply worked in a barn once," Professor Kirby remarked.

Peter's eyes darted anywhere, trying not to take in Dr. Kirby's intense and curious stare. "I'd better get back to work," he said, backing away. "Mr. Dixon will be looking for me."

He could feel their stares on his back as he walked away. What on earth was the matter with him? He had tried so carefully to avoid horses and young ladies, and in the past two days he'd been in close contact with both. *Why are You leading me this direction, Lord? Don't You know me? Lead me away from this. Lead me in paths of righteousness.* When his feet hit gravel, he looked up in surprise. He'd been so intent on his prayer, he took no note of where he was going and realized that he'd made his way to the road that ran in front of Dr. Kirby's house. He still needed to go to Dr. Tuttle's and finish the work he'd started. Wheels in need of some oil made him look up. A horse-drawn streetcar stopped on the opposite side of High Street. Several people got out, including a woman in a dark cloak and bonnet. A bonnet? He hadn't seen anyone wear a bonnet since he was a child. Once she crossed the street, the woman pulled off the hat, and to his surprise, it was Anne Kirby. She walked toward the house with lowered eyes, her face more melancholy than usual. Curious, he waited for her to approach.

"Miss Kirby?" She looked up and the astonishment in her eyes was tempered by the redness of recent tears. "Are you all right? You're not hurt are you?"

"Mr. Ward." She paused, glancing away before looking at him again. "I'm fine. What are you doing here?"

Peter blinked. "I was working next door at Dr. Tuttle's house when I heard a commotion. Your uncle's horse threw him—"

"What?" She raised her hand to her chest.

"Your uncle's all right. But I think he might have hurt his arm somehow."

"What about Scioto?"

Peter stared at her for a moment. "I'm afraid it looks like he sprained a tendon. Dr. Townshend is here, too. He's already suggested a poultice."

She rushed past him and flew up the steps to the house. "Thank you, Mr. Ward," she called back.

"You're welcome." But she was inside before he finished speaking the words. He shook his head and turned toward the Tuttle residence to retrieve his tools. What was she doing, getting off the streetcar alone and dressed in a cloak and bonnet? According to Mike, the streetcar went into Columbus. Well, maybe she hadn't gone far, perhaps only a few blocks to visit a friend. But that didn't make sense. Why pay streetcar fare when she could walk? And if she had been visiting a friend, why would she return close to tears?

Peter quickly finished the minor repair to Professor Tuttle's home and gathered his tools. As he walked to the Main Building, an uneasy thought crossed his mind. Just how disgraceful had this Sam McAllister's conduct been toward Miss Kirby? Surely she wasn't in the same state as Letty Jamison. But her sadness and her behavior today offered no other explanation. He strangled the handle of his tool bag and curled his other hand into an iron-like fist. No wonder the professor had wanted to beat the living daylights out of the man. But wait. If that were the case, certainly her pa would have already forced the young man to marry her. Recalling the face of Jonah Kirby in the professor's wedding picture, he could tell he was hardly a man to be crossed. Then it hit him. *They don't know.* It all made sense—her tears, the cloak and bonnet. She'd been in town to visit a doctor.

The weight of that thought stopped him cold. He ran his free hand through his hair as another question seared its way through his head. Had she given up her virtue willingly or had it been stolen from her? His gut told him it had to be the latter. A woman could not possess such innocent eyes and be some sort of siren. It made sense, too. She hadn't said anything to avoid embarrassment and was now finding herself in an even worse situation. The blame for that sort of thing always seemed to fall on the woman, which Peter had always found to be monstrously unfair. During his time on the road and in the finest homes in Pittsburgh, he knew from experience that was not always the case.

He started on his way again and found himself wondering if that might have been the case with Letty. But why had she said he was responsible? He shook his head. It didn't really matter now. After all this time, her father would have either sent her somewhere out of state or found someone else to marry her. In spite of her dishonesty, he found himself praying everything would turn out for the best. At least her prospects were more hopeful than Anne Kirby's. If he were right about her, he felt he needed to find some way to help.

In the distance Peter saw Mike coming from the boiler house behind the Main Building and he waved to him. As he drew closer, he saw someone approach his boss. He frowned. It was Harvey Pryce.

"Mr. Cope asked me to give these to you," Peter heard him say as he approached. "Couldn't help but notice some of those bills are past due."

Mike took the bundle of papers and gave him a look. "These papers are between me and the board."

Harvey shrugged. "He also happened to ask me if I was working for you this term. I told him you already had someone." Noticing Peter, he gave him a nasty smile. "I knew I recognized you before. I guess our 'lesson' didn't mess you up too bad."

Peter stared at him for a second as his full meaning sunk in. Then he dropped his bag and lunged at Harvey. He was stopped by Mike's arm across his shoulders.

"Whoa, Pete! What's going on?"

"He was with those boys who beat me," he said. He'd told Mike about his timber lesson when he hired him. "I wasn't hurting anyone. Why'd you pick on me?"

"It was my job, keeping tramps like you from hitching free rides," Harvey replied. "Handing out timber lessons was working until you showed up. My boss found out and fired me."

"I ought to have you arrested," Mike said.

Peter opened his mouth to agree but stopped himself. If he had to testify against Harvey, it might draw unwanted attention. What if his uncle was still looking for him? Peter didn't put it past him for a second that he might want to find him out of sheer spite. His departure had most assuredly caused his uncle a great deal of embarrassment.

"No." Peter said. "I'd rather put that behind me."

Mike stared at him. "You sure?"

"Yes."

Mike lowered his arm and looked at Harvey. "I think it's time you left."

Pryce's face turned smug. "Yeah it is, now that you

mention it. I have to pack. Finally got me a job." He walked off.

Peter hoped it would be a long time before he saw Harvey Pryce again.

Anne watched as Uncle Daniel paced in front of the parlor mantel after listening carefully to the news Patrick Howard had given him concerning Scioto. It had been a full day since Scioto's injury, and Professor Townshend had sent the young man over to see how the poultice was doing. He had not given them good news.

"Why isn't it working?" her uncle asked.

"Sir, your man hasn't been applying it," Mr. Howard replied.

Uncle Daniel stopped and stared at him.

"Why not?" Anne asked.

"He told me it wouldn't work. He said all the horse needs is rest and a little liniment." Mr. Howard scowled. "But I can't find any evidence that he's even been applying that."

Anne watched her uncle's knuckles turn snow white as he clenched his fist and tapped it against his leg. His other arm was in a sling. It was fortunate that her uncle had only severely sprained his shoulder when Scioto threw him. And at the moment, fortunate for Ben, too. Her uncle looked like he wanted to throttle him.

"Please be so kind as to ask Ben to come inside, Patrick," he said after taking one more turn in front of the fireplace.

Mr. Howard left and Anne watched her uncle resume his pacing. She was as worried about Scioto as he was—perhaps even more—but she couldn't help but feel glad that all the fuss had kept Mr. Howard from asking about her "injured" foot. The questions it would raise would inevitably lead to her uncle finding out where she'd gone yesterday. She squirmed as she thought of how she had deceived both of them, but she hadn't seen any other way around it. *I'm sorry, Lord. Please forgive me. I'll tell Uncle Daniel what I did eventually. Just not yet.*

A few minutes later, a frightened-looking Ben stood before all three of them, twisting what might have been a hat in both hands. He looked so wretched that Anne couldn't help feeling sorry for him. Her uncle must have, as well, for his voice held only a slight edge.

"Would you care to explain why my horse is still suffering almost a day after his injury?"

Ben refused to look at any of them. "I can't really get near him, sir."

Her uncle looked at her then back at Ben. "But you've been caring for him for almost a month and a half now. You told me weeks ago he was behaving for you."

"I know, sir. I'm sorry; I really am. I just wanted this job so bad."

"You should have said something," Anne said. Tears rose in her eyes as she thought about how neglected Scioto must have felt. If only she hadn't avoided seeing him for so long.

"If you can't go near him, then how was it he looked so well yesterday?" Mr. Howard asked.

"I got up real early. It took me 'til first light to get him ready and saddled."

Her uncle drew in a long breath. "I'm afraid I'll have to let you go, Ben."

The young man's shoulders slumped and his hands fell to his sides. "Yes, sir, I'll go clear my things." He turned to go, but Uncle Daniel spoke again.

"Your family isn't from Columbus, are they?"

"No, sir, we're from Celina."

"If you decide you want to go back home instead of finding work here, please come see me. I'll see that you get home."

The news appeared to lighten Ben's load a little. "Thank you, sir."

"We need to apply the poultice immediately," Patrick said after Ben left. "I wonder if you could help me."

"Of course," Anne replied, rising from her seat.

Patrick raised his eyebrows. "Thank you, Miss Kirby, but I was speaking to your uncle." He turned to him. "Scioto wasn't very happy with me either, sir. I know it might be difficult with your arm—"

"He should be fine if I'm holding on to his halter." Uncle Daniel gave Anne a sympathetic glance. "Ask Mrs. Werner to heat up some water."

"Not to boiling though," Patrick said.

"I'm familiar with the poultice Dr. Townshend recommended, Mr. Howard," Anne said, frowning slightly. "If you'll excuse me, I'll go speak with her now."

A few hours later, she and her uncle stood outside Scioto's stall as Anne tried not to fume over the slow, careful way Patrick had explained to her how to continue with the poultice. He'd left for his boardinghouse moments ago. Anne must have had a sour look on her face since her uncle chuckled.

"You're sure you got all that now?" he mimicked. Anne gave him such a withering look that he held his free hand up as if to forestall a blow. "I must admit he went a little overboard."

Scioto lowered his head toward Anne, and she laid her hand across his nose. "I should never have stopped visiting him."

"And I should have made more time to do so." Uncle Daniel rubbed the horse's neck. "We'll let him rest for the time being."

Anne nodded. She needed to go in and heat more water to keep the poultice warm. "Who will take care of him now?" she asked as they walked to the house.

"Mr. Howard said he'd make enquiries, but he wasn't very hopeful," her uncle replied. "He said he'd do it himself, but his studies won't allow him the time."

"We can't move him," she said carefully. "With your arm and teaching schedule, you doing the job is out of the question, and Mrs. Werner is not particularly fond of horses." She looked up hopefully at her uncle.

A deep frown creased his face. "I don't like it, Anne. I promised your pa."

"I know, but considering the circumstances, I don't think he'd object." Anne waited through a long pause. She was eventually rewarded for her patience.

"I don't see how we have much choice." He looked over his glasses at her. "I know you'll take good care of him, but it will only be until I can hire someone."

His gaze turned thoughtful. "In fact I may not have to look far."

Anne didn't let his last few words spoil her delight. She squeezed his good arm. "I understand. Thank you, Uncle Daniel."

Chapter 8

"This is all my fault." Peter sat on his cot and watched his boss pack his things.

"Don't blame yourself, Pete," Mike said as he worked. "I don't."

"But you never would have lost your job if you hadn't hired me. You said the board wasn't happy about it."

Mike stopped packing and rubbed the back of his neck. "That's not it, exactly." He sat down on the cot next to Peter. "I kind of got myself in this mess."

"What do you mean?"

"Those bills Harvey gave me a few weeks ago were supposed to be paid by me. Then the board was to re-imburse me." He paused, looking more than a little embarrassed. "I sorta forgot about them. And this hasn't

been the first time. The bills went past due and got sent
to the board. Again."

"Ah, Mike." Peter said sadly. "I wish you had told
me. I could have helped you remember."

"Well, that's not all. Before you came I told the
board how much money I needed for this term, and
they gave me enough for two assistants." He looked at
Peter. "When Dr. Kirby spoke to me about you, I felt
real sorry for you. So I paid you salary for two men."

Peter ran a hand through his hair. He'd always wondered if his pay was too high, but since he'd never
worked for someone before he'd never questioned Mike
about it. Now he wished he had. A knock sounded at
the door and they looked at each other.

"I still don't believe they hired him," Peter said.

"I tried to tell them." Mike rose wearily to answer
the door.

Harvey Pryce walked in with his friend Frank. Both
men were loaded down with wooden crates. "Humph,"
Harvey said as he took in the one-room cabin. "Not
much, but it'll do."

"It keeps the rain off your head." Mike continued
with his packing.

"I guess." Harvey set down his crate and looked at
Peter. "What are you still doing here?"

"Don't worry, I'll be gone by the morning," Peter
said.

"I wanted to try and convince you to keep him on,"
Mike said as he stuffed the last of his things in an old
carpetbag. "He knows how things work around here."

"I'm pretty sure I can handle it," Harvey said.

Peter couldn't stop the chuckle that escaped his lips. Harvey glared at him.

"I would've had this job sooner if me and the boys had given you a better lesson."

Peter stood, his fists clenched tight. "Maybe it's time I give *you* a lesson."

"Pete," Mike warned. "Don't do it."

"Ah come on, Pete," Pryce taunted. "Let's have at it."

Common sense quickly prevailing, he turned away from Harvey. "No. It's not worth it."

Harvey sneered at him then nudged Frank, who had also set down his crate. "Let's go get something to drink. We'll bring the rest of my stuff over tomorrow."

"You start tomorrow," Mike retorted. "How are you going to move in and do what needs done around here?"

"That's my business," Harvey said as he and Frank walked out the door.

Peter shook his head. "He really has no idea what he's getting into."

Mike nodded in agreement and set the carpetbag near the door, along with the rest of his things. "I guess that's it for me." He held out his hand and Peter shook it. "I'm sorry they don't need you over at the shop."

"That's all right. I'll find something." As Peter spoke, a wagon pulled up outside.

"That'd be the fellas for me," Mike said.

Peter followed him over to the door, picked up some of his things, and followed him outside. A couple of Mike's friends had driven over to help him move to a boardinghouse near Columbus Machine Company, where he'd found a job. They jumped down and Mike introduced them. "This is Geoff Evans and Steve Brock."

"Sorry to hear about your job." Steve shook Peter's hand. "I think there might be an opening where I work. I can check and come by and get you tomorrow if you like. It'd be around lunchtime. Think you'll be here?"

Mike smirked. "Harvey wants him gone by the time he comes back tomorrow. But he and Frank went out drinking. Pete will be here."

They laughed and soon had all of Mike's things in the back of the wagon. "I'll see if there's a room at the boardinghouse," Mike said as he climbed up. "I know the fella Steve works for. More than likely, you'll have a job come tomorrow."

Peter shook his hand. "Thanks, Mike. For everything."

As the wagon rolled off, Peter stood outside, looking at the fading sky. A new job in the city would be an answer to prayer. He needed to leave the university. Dr. Kirby had been forced to fire his stable boy and had offered the job to Peter. As much as he wanted to accept it, he knew he shouldn't. Then there was Anne Kirby. As much as he wanted to help her, there just didn't seem to be a proper way to go about it. It also didn't help that the few times he'd seen her in the last month she hadn't seemed any better, at least in unguarded moments. She seemed normal enough when she was with her uncle, but on the few occasions he'd checked the pipes in the library, he'd caught glimpses of her dabbing her eyes. *Lord, You know all things and*

You know this situation she's in. Lead her to someone that can help her. Restore her soul.

A brisk gust sent him back into the house, and he put more wood in the stove. The weather had been unpredictable. The days had been pleasant enough, but the nights had been getting quite cold, at least to Peter's way of thinking. He'd never liked being cold. He put another piece in for good measure then set about packing up what few things he had and making sure the log house was more or less in order. Lately Peter had been reading a passage in Romans about enemies. If being nice to Harvey Pryce meant that "coals of fire" would be heaped on his head, so much the better. He only wished he could do a few nice things for Uncle Randall and his cousin Edward.

He pushed the woodbox closer to the stove. What about his grandfather? Did he desire the same thing for him? As much as he thought the answer should be "yes," his heart didn't agree. In the end, Granddad's cutting him off had been a good thing. He was a better man now. The thought made him shake his head at himself. Was he really? He'd just wished the worst for three different people. When Dr. Kirby first pointed out that passage to him after Peter had been injured, he'd been quick to say it wasn't about revenge. It was about forgiveness. *That's something You'll have to help me with, Lord. Forgiving them just isn't on my heart right yet.* He set the last few things in order and fell into bed, not bothering to remove his clothes. The one blanket he had wasn't exactly the warmest.

It was the heat that woke Peter later. Heat and the light from the raging fire that flickered up the wall opposite his bed. It had begun to spread to a good portion of the roof as well. He ran out the door, yelling for help. Several figures were running toward him from the direction of the student boardinghouse, some carrying buckets.

"Come on," one of them shouted. "We'll form a bucket brigade from the lake to here."

"What about the fire department?" Peter yelled as they started for it.

"They'll be here soon. We already sent someone to the signal box." The student stopped and looked around in alarm. "Where's Mike?"

"He's not here." Peter pulled on his arm. "Come on!"

But their buckets might as well have been thimbles. By the time they formed the line, flames engulfed the whole building. All they could do was make sure the fire didn't spread. It was only after the fire department arrived with its steam-powered pumper that they finally took a break. Peter slumped on the ground, head in his hands, coughing from the smoke. How on earth had this happened?

"Where is he? He's got to be here somewhere."

Peter looked up. Harvey Pryce strode up to the scene, a police officer on his heels. He spotted Peter and immediately made his way over. "There he is. Arrest him!"

Peter jumped to his feet. "What?"

"Now Mr. Pryce, let's just wait a minute," the officer said. "We don't even know if this was an accident or what."

"It's no accident," Harvey said. "This guy has a grudge against me because I got his boss's job. He took a swing at me earlier tonight, gave me a sore jaw. Now he's burned down my house out of spite."

"That's not what happened!" Peter yelled.

The students that had formed the bucket brigade wandered over to watch.

"I have a witness," Harvey declared. "My friend Frank Morris saw the whole thing."

"I—" Peter began. The policeman took hold of his arm. "Wait, I didn't do anything."

"I've heard enough to know that this needs to go before the court." The officer slapped handcuffs on him. "You're going down to the city prison for the time being."

Peter soon found himself confined to a small cell with several other men. Since it was the middle of the night most of them were asleep or, judging from the smell, passed out from too much liquor. One or two woke up when he was let in, but he quietly made his way to the back of the cell and ignored their insults and veiled threats. A low stone ledge ran beneath the window and he climbed up on it. He couldn't even contemplate the idea of sitting on the floor.

He moved into the corner and, leaning back, drew his knees up. Scrunching his eyes shut, he tried to wake himself up from the nightmare he found himself in. But the stench of the cell and the smoke that hung heavily to his clothes and beard told him he was wide awake. Not to mention the cold breeze that blew in from the window. Bars were the only thing that covered the square slit near the top of the cell. When he rested his head against the wall he could see a bare sliver of the night sky. He stared at it, not quite sure what to think or even what to pray.

After about a quarter of an hour, he closed his eyes. *I'm sorry I let Harvey provoke me, Lord. I shouldn't have said anything.* He wondered what the judge would say. According to the jailer who had led him to the cell, he'd go to court sometime tomorrow. How was he going to get out of this? The only person who knew that Harvey was lying was Mike, and he had no way of getting a hold of him. And what if they decided he started the fire? *But I didn't do it. I didn't do anything to start that fire.* He wondered if Harvey had started it on purpose. He couldn't imagine why. He hadn't even liked the place. Was he worried that he would still try to arrest him for having him beaten? Peter shook his head. Whatever the reason, it certainly didn't matter now.

A commotion drew his attention to the cell door, where a man was forced inside. He fell on top of a rough-looking fellow who'd been leaning against the bars, sleeping. He cursed and kicked him off. The man tumbled to the ground, and Peter jumped up to help him.

"Hey, are you all right?" he whispered. He squinted at the man's face in the dim light. "Uncle Billy?"

"Petey!" the man exclaimed. A couple of men cursed and shushed them, and Peter immediately hauled his friend to his spot at the back of the cell.

"Hey now, Lieutenant," Uncle Billy said. "You watch yourself there. I'm your superior officer, remember?"

Peter smiled inwardly. How could he have forgotten Billy's...eccentricities? He stood up straight and gave him a quick salute. "Sorry, sir. What are you doing here?"

"Them Rebs got me." He shook his head. "They tried to take the general away from me."

"Is he all right, sir?"

Uncle Billy grinned as he reached his hand into the pocket of his threadbare Union jacket. When he pulled it out, there in his hand was a small brown field mouse. "Them Rebs won't get General Grant that easy."

Peter nodded and smiled. Uncle Billy had kept him company many times during his tramping days. Or rather, Peter had kept Uncle Billy company. He'd first met him in Circleville, a little town south of Columbus, and he wasn't popular with the other transients. His ramblings about the War Between the States and his unshakable belief that he was General William T. Sherman made them uncomfortable. Then there was the mouse he carried around in his pocket, which he insisted was General Ulysses S. Grant. Peter had felt sorry for him and befriended him. The war still rested heavily on his mind, but all in all, he was a kindhearted soul. The only time he became violent was when anyone tried to go after his mouse. "I'm glad their latest attempt to capture General Grant was unsuccessful," he said, patting Billy on the back.

The man raised the mouse up to his face. "He's worried about the next campaign. See how he's pacing?" He looked at Peter. "You know anything that'd sooth the general?"

Peter smiled. "Yes, sir." He knew just the thing. God had placed it on his heart to memorize over a month ago. He helped Uncle Billy up on the ledge and hopped up next to him.

"The Lord is my shepherd, I shall not want," he quoted softly. "He maketh me to lie down in green pastures. He leadeth me beside the still waters. He restoreth my soul..."

Chapter 9

"Thank you for letting me eat with you and Anne today, Dr. Kirby," Emma said.

Uncle Daniel smiled at her from behind his office desk as she and Anne laid cloths out on it and unpacked their lunch baskets. "We're glad to have you join us, Miss Long. Although, I have to wonder who is taking care of the library right now. I thought you two took turns keeping an eye on things during lunch."

"Normally we do," Anne replied with a smile. "But there are so few people who come into the library at this hour, we decided we could probably get away with leaving a note on the door explaining where we are."

"I hope no one comes looking for us," Emma said, laying out her ham sandwich. "Or we'll be in for a short lunch."

"Oh it can't be that someone will need both of us.

I'll go if someone comes." Anne handed her uncle a boiled egg, along with a small paper packet of salt.

"Thank you, Anne." Emma brought a couple of chairs forward for them to sit in. "I'm going to miss you come January."

"So you've heard from Miss Fuller?" Uncle Daniel asked.

"Yes, Clara says she'll be back at the start of winter term."

"Then that means you'll have to find a new position, Anne." Her uncle smiled at her. "Have you started looking yet?"

Anne nodded. "Yes, I've written a few letters." She took a bite of her sandwich so she wouldn't have to elaborate. She'd sent several letters, all to districts out west. A small school district outside Topeka, Kansas, had recently replied, offering her a job. Their letter requested her to start at her earliest convenience. All she needed to do was make the arrangements, but that would take another trip into Columbus. She laid her sandwich down—the thought had made it suddenly taste like shoe leather. But it had to be done. She glanced at her uncle, trying to remember when he'd said his next faculty meeting would take place. Hopefully it would be soon.

"I heard you found a new stable man," Emma said between bites of her sandwich.

"Yes," Uncle Daniel answered, his glance sliding toward Anne. "A very well-trained individual, but it's only temporary, I'm afraid."

Anne looked down, concentrating on peeling her hardboiled egg. She'd been so glad to take charge of

Scioto again. It had been hard not talking to anyone about her troubles over the past month, but opening up to him hadn't been the same as it had been at home. Instead of feeling better, she felt worse. She couldn't understand it. She felt God nudging her to talk to Him. *Why, Father? What more is there to say?*

Someone knocked on the door and Emma groaned.

"I'll see who it is," Anne said. Instead of the student she'd anticipated seeing, Mike Dixon stood before her. Uncle Daniel caught sight of him and rose from his seat.

"Hello, Mike." Her uncle joined her at the door. "We were so sorry to hear you'd been let go."

"Yes, we'll miss you Mike," Anne said, and Emma, leaning back to catch a glimpse of the janitor, echoed the sentiment.

Mike nodded. "Thank you. Dr. Kirby, I was wondering if I might speak to you in private."

Anne looked at her uncle. "Do you want Emma and me to leave for a moment?"

"No, of course not. We'll just step out into the hall." He smiled and shut the door behind him.

"I wonder what that's about," Emma wondered aloud.

"Maybe he wants to use my uncle as a reference." Anne sat back down.

"That can't be; I've heard he has a job." She wiped her hands on a cloth napkin and folded up the paper from her sandwich. "Did you hear the bells from the fire engine last night?"

"Yes! They went right past our house," she replied.

The janitor's house burning down last night had been the talk of the students all morning.

"A few of the fellows from George Smart's boardinghouse ran out to help."

Anne's eyebrows rose. "How do you know?"

"George stopped by the library this morning just to tell me." She blushed.

"I'm glad for you. He seems like a nice young man. Although I'm surprised he didn't go, too."

"He would have, but he was away visiting family." She cocked her head at Anne. "Patrick Howard is a pretty nice fellow, too."

Anne frowned. "I know."

"I still don't understand why you chased him away." Emma looked at her reprovingly. "You couldn't ask for a better man."

Anne was saved from replying by the sudden reappearance of her uncle. "I'm afraid there's an emergency that needs my attention." He shrugged into his suit jacket and handed Anne a key. "Lock up my office and place a sign on my door. I'll have to cancel my afternoon classes."

"What's wrong?" she asked. The look of concern on his face alarmed her. "It's not Scioto, is it?"

"No, my dear, he's fine. I'll explain later. Hopefully I'll be home by dinner."

Throughout the long night, Peter silently repeated Psalm 23 to himself. He spent the morning keeping Uncle Billy out of trouble with their cellmates. Not long after lunch, they were all ushered to a closed police wagon to be taken to the courthouse. The psalm had kept Peter's heart at ease until he asked the police officer who rode with them about the judge they were soon to face.

"The mayor is the police and judge," he said gruffly.

"What's he like?"

"He won't go easy on you if he thinks you're guilty. Now be quiet."

Uncle Billy glared at the officer. "You watch yourself! That's my lieutenant you're talking to."

"And who are you supposed to be?"

"I'm General William Tecumseh Sherman." The officer and the other prisoners laughed. "Don't believe me? General Grant will confirm it." The old man reached into his pocket, but Peter quickly stopped him.

"The general needs his rest, sir."

Uncle Billy didn't look pleased but left the mouse in his pocket, much to Peter's relief.

His heart pounded as they were marched into the courtroom. Mayor Walcutt was a gruff-looking man with a long goatee, a mustache, and a stern eye. But as he worked through the cases brought before him, Peter saw that he was a fair-minded man, only fining or imprisoning those who truly deserved it. The man right before him had beaten his wife in a drunken stupor. The woman came before the judge to plead on her husband's behalf, but Mayor Walcutt wasn't swayed. His eyes turned to black coals as he stared down at the man, saying, "I only wish it were within my power to sentence you to the same beating you gave this woman who came to intercede for you."

Peter's case was called, and as he walked up to stand before the mayor, he glanced out over the gallery. Harvey Pryce was there, along with Frank Morris, but Mike Dixon's and Professor Kirby's presence surprised Peter. He felt both relieved and mortified. Mike would certainly tell the judge the truth, but Peter wanted to hide in shame from Dr. Kirby. What must the professor think of him?

"Mr. Peter Ward?"

Peter looked up at the judge's stern face. "Yes, sir."

"You've been accused of assault and burning down a log house belonging to The Ohio State University." The mayor's eyebrows drew together. "How do you plead?"

"Not guilty, sir."

The mayor looked down at the papers before him. "Mr. Harvey Pryce, please step forward."

Harvey did as he was told. "Yes, your honor?"

"Tell me exactly what happened."

"Well, I've recently been hired as janitor up at the university. Frank and I were moving my things into the janitor's cabin when Ward here starts getting nasty and hits me."

The mayor took a long look at him. "Is that how you got the bruise on your jaw?"

"Yes, hurts like the devil, too."

"And you have a witness who can verify this?"

Harvey motioned to Frank. "Yes, sir." He looked back at his friend, who hadn't moved, and said, "Come on, tell the judge what happened."

But Frank looked from Harvey to Peter then to the mayor and got up and walked out of the courtroom. Someone cleared his throat, and Peter turned. Both Mike and Dr. Kirby had risen from their seats. "If you will forgive me, Mayor Walcutt, Mr. Dixon and I would like to speak on Mr. Ward's behalf."

Frowning at Harvey, the mayor nodded. "I think that would be very helpful, Mr.—?"

"I am Dr. Daniel Kirby, a professor at The Ohio State University. This is Michael Dixon, who, until recently, was the janitor for the university."

The mayor listened carefully as Mike described exactly what happened the night before, and what Harvey had said and done to provoke Peter. "I won't lie and say Pete didn't want to let him have it, but he never touched Harvey."

"Then how did Mr. Pryce get his bruised jaw?" Mayor Walcutt asked.

"Him and Frank decided to go drinking last night, your honor. We both heard him suggest it to Frank before they left the cabin."

"I see." The mayor looked at Harvey, who was looking anywhere but up at him. "Very well, I'm satisfied that Mr. Ward did not hit Mr. Pryce. But there is the burning of the log house to consider."

"I can vouch for this young man's character in that regard," Dr. Kirby said firmly. "He has been a guest in my home and I am convinced he would not do such a thing."

"Oh no," Peter blurted out. He'd replayed over and over in his mind everything he'd done last night and suddenly realized what happened. He felt the blood leave his face. "I think I started the fire."

Dr. Kirby looked at him, incredulously. "What do you mean?"

Peter locked eyes with Mike. "It was so stupid of

me. After you left, I got cold. I put a couple of logs on the fire, and while I was straightening up, I—I think I moved the woodbox too close to the stove. Then I fell asleep." How could he have been so stupid? Mike had warned him about putting anything flammable too close to the stove, in case it overheated. He looked up at the judge. "It was an accident."

The mayor looked carefully at him. "I believe you, son. But I will need to hear what the fire captain says." He looked at Professor Kirby. "I will release him to you, Dr. Kirby."

"Thank you, sir," he replied. "I am confident you will find everything just as Mr. Ward described."

Peter's hands shook with relief as the bailiff removed the handcuffs. He looked up to thank the mayor but found the gentleman looking at Harvey.

"Mr. Pryce," the mayor said. "I should have you arrested for what Mr. Dixon just told me about you giving Mr. Ward a timber lesson."

Harvey looked up at the judge, his dark eyes wide.

"Sir, please," Peter said. "I'm fine now. Let Mr. Pryce go."

"This man should be brought to justice, Peter," Dr. Kirby said.

"I know, sir." But it wasn't the desire to remain anonymous that moved Peter now. He felt God nudging him to show Harvey the same mercy as the professor had shown him. "I haven't always been the man I am now. I was given a second chance, sir. Harvey deserves one as well."

"Admirable, young man, admirable," the mayor said. "Consider yourself lucky, Mr. Pryce."

Harvey looked so angry, Peter thought he might burst into flame. But he only glared at him, saying nothing, as he rose and stalked out of the courtroom. Dr. Kirby, Mike, and Peter started to leave when Uncle Billy's name was called.

Peter stopped short of the courtroom door and looked back. His friend shuffled up in front of the judge and pulled off his worn forage cap.

"Is Uncle Billy your real name?" the mayor asked.

"Well, no sir," Billy said. "That's what the men call me. My name is William Tecumseh Sherman."

Peter quickly strode forward but not in time to stop his friend from pulling out "General Grant." Mayor Walcutt's eyes grew large and a woman in the gallery screeched.

"Sir, please, I don't know what the charges are against him——" Peter began.

"He bit me," said a voice from the gallery. A man with a bandaged hand stood up. "He brought that vermin into my saloon, waving him around, asking people to buy a cigar and a drink for 'General Grant' there."

"That Reb tried to capture the general!" Uncle Billy exclaimed.

Peter shook his head. He'd done that again? "Sir, please, he doesn't really know what he's doing."

"That much is clear," the mayor said. "Do you know his real name?"

"Give me just a moment, sir." Peter gave Uncle Billy a salute. "General, do you have your papers on you?" Peter had thought he'd seen Uncle Billy with official-looking documents on more than one occasion but had never gotten a good look at them. He prayed he still had them.

Uncle Billy looked doubtfully at him. "Why do you need my papers, Lieutenant?"

"I don't, sir, but this gentleman does." Uncle Billy's frown deepened, and Peter grasped for an explanation. "It's...official business, sir. Spies have been seen in the area."

Slowly, the old man pulled a worn set of papers from inside his shirt. He handed them to Peter, who handed them to the bailiff. Mayor Walcutt took them and read the name he found written there.

"Harold Albert Cooper, sergeant for the Union Army, discharged June 1865."

The words had a dramatic effect on Billy. He began to shake uncontrollably and raised his hand to his forehead. His eyes swam, and he looked miserable and confused. Peter's heart tightened and he laid his hand on his friend's back. Dr. Kirby walked forward.

"Mayor, under the circumstances, I don't think a normal sentence is called for." The professor's face was even graver than his voice.

"You're right, Professor," Mayor Walcutt replied. "Anything else would be an insult to the men I commanded in the war." The mayor looked up at the man Billy had assaulted, who nodded agreement, but Peter didn't care for the fear and distrust in the man's face. It wasn't as if Uncle Billy could help what was wrong with him.

"I'll send word to Dr. Finch and see what can be done." The mayor nodded to the bailiff, who gently took Uncle Billy out a side door.

Dr. Kirby, his hand on Peter's arm, guided him to the door. "Who is Dr. Finch, sir?" Peter asked. "He's not the poorhouse doctor, is he?"

"No," the professor replied, his eyes thoughtful. "Dr. Finch is the superintendent of the Columbus Asylum for the Insane. You can be sure your friend is in good hands." He took a deep breath, and then looked at Peter. "Now, young man, we have a great deal to discuss."

Chapter 10

"Good afternoon, Miss Kirby. How is Scioto doing?"

Anne looked toward the voice. Patrick Howard stood at the bottom of the steps of the Main Building.

Sighing inwardly, she made her way down to join him. "He's doing very well, Mr. Howard."

"It's fortunate your uncle found someone to care for him so quickly. But he didn't mention who it was."

Anne bit the inside of her lip before answering. "Oh—it's someone who came down from Ostrander a few months ago." She held her breath, hoping he wouldn't ask more. To spare Anne's reputation, Uncle Daniel hadn't wanted it known that she was performing a man's job.

"A family friend, then?"

"Yes," she answered brightly.

He nodded and looked behind her toward the door.

"Where is your uncle this afternoon? Don't you usually walk home together?"

"Yes, we do. He was called away around lunchtime. Some sort of emergency, but he didn't say what it was."

"I hope it wasn't anything serious," Mr. Howard said. "Do you think it had something to do with the fire at the janitor's house last night?"

Anne blinked. "I wouldn't think so. But—"

"But what?"

"Well, Mike Dixon came to speak to him just before he left."

Patrick Howard nodded. "Then it must be about the fire."

"Why do you say that?"

"Because I heard they arrested the janitor's assistant for it," he explained. "Didn't your uncle help him get the job?"

"Yes, he did." Anne brows furrowed. Why on earth would Mr. Ward burn down the janitor's house? She knew he'd lost his job when Mike lost his, but she had never imagined him capable of something so violent. She shrugged. "I'll find out when I get home. He's sure to be back by now."

"Would you like me to escort you? I can make sure the new man is treating Scioto properly."

Anne gritted her teeth as she reminded herself that Mr. Howard had no idea who the "new man" was. "No, thank you. It's not a very long walk, and I can assure you that Scioto is just fine."

Mr. Howard looked resigned. "I see," he said. Stiffly, he tipped his bowler hat. "Please give your uncle my regards."

Anne watched Mr. Howard walk south toward his boardinghouse. One more young man finally chased away. Tears pricked at her eyes as she wondered if she shouldn't reconsider everything. Was spinsterhood her only option? Memories of last month's visit to Columbus sharply asserted themselves. No, for everyone's sake, this had to be done. Besides, how could she court, or especially marry, someone without telling him the truth about herself? *You tried that with Sam, remember? See how that turned out?*

Dusk began to fall as she walked into the house. She poked her head into the kitchen, and Mrs. Werner told her Uncle Daniel was out back with "that horse of his." Chuckling, Anne went to change, eager to make her way to the stable. Even though her conversations with Scioto weren't as helpful as they used to be, working in the stable was still something of a balm.

Uncle Daniel was standing outside Scioto's stall when she came in. "Good afternoon, my dear."

"Hello," she said, giving him a hug. "Now, what was all the fuss about today?" She checked Scioto's feed bin. It was empty and she looked inquiringly at her uncle.

"He's already been fed," he replied with a slight smile.

Anne walked to the tack room and returned with the grooming kit.

"I was called away to the courthouse."

"The courthouse?" Anne let herself in the stall. Scioto gently nudged her in greeting. She slid his halter on and secured the lead. "Why? Did it have to do with the fire at the janitor's house?"

"As a matter of fact, it did."

She was about to ask what happened when she ran her hand over Scioto's coat. Turning, she looked at her uncle in consternation. "Don't tell me you groomed him as well? I thought your arm was still a little stiff."

"It is."

"Then who groomed him?"

"I did."

Anne stepped out of the stall. A handsome young man came down the stairs that led to the stableman's chambers above. He was wiping his freshly shaven face with a towel and his chocolate brown hair looked as if it had been recently trimmed. He flung the towel over his shoulder, his green eyes taking hold of hers. She stared at him, struggling to figure out just where she'd seen those eyes before.

"Anne," her uncle said. "Surely you remember Mr. Ward."

"Mr. Ward?" she breathed. No, it couldn't be. Could it? Was it possible that all that hair had covered up such a handsome face?

He smiled, and Anne thought her heart would stop from sheer exhaustion. "At your service, Miss Kirby; as you can see, I do more than kill spiders."

His meaning quickly shot through her addled thoughts and brought them to order. She frowned. Handsome or not, why was *he* doing *her* job? And him a criminal! She crossed her arms. "I thought you also swept rooms and fixed gas pipes, not to mention burning down houses."

Her uncle frowned. "Anne."

"Patrick Howard told me they arrested him last night for burning down Mike's house!"

"The charges were dropped," Uncle Daniel replied sternly. "Mike came to get me today because he knew Mr. Ward was innocent and wanted me to speak with him on Mr. Ward's behalf."

"Then how did it burn down?"

"It was an accident," Mr. Ward replied. "I'm afraid I left the woodbox too close to the stove. I fell asleep, and the stove overheated." He looked at her uncle with sincere eyes. "I can assure you that won't happen here, sir."

Uncle Daniel smiled and patted him on the shoulder. "Of course not; I know you'll take good care of Scioto."

"But he's a janitor, Uncle Daniel," Anne countered.

"Actually, Mr. Ward is a man of many talents," her uncle said. "Ones that will no longer go untapped." Anne saw the look he and Mr. Ward exchanged.

"Yes, sir." Mr. Ward smiled slightly. He turned his green gaze to her once more. "I have to compliment you, Miss Kirby. You've done a good job."

"Yes, Anne was very thorough," her uncle said. "I'm sure she'll be relieved to have the responsibility taken out of her hands." Anne swung around to look at him. "You do remember agreeing you'd do the job only until a replacement could be found."

"Yes, but—"

"Now, I believe Mrs. Werner is nearly finished with dinner and I'm famished," her uncle said before she could protest further. "It's been a long day."

Anne, watching Mr. Ward walk into Scioto's stall and pick up the grooming bucket, felt a slight sense of betrayal as the horse nudged him just as he'd done to her a few minutes earlier. He smiled, and she saw the regard he already held for the animal as he gently stroked Scioto's neck. He put the grooming kit away then held the door open for her and her uncle and followed them out.

She was surprised and more than curious that her uncle insisted Mr. Ward eat with them. Ben had always eaten with Mrs. Werner in the kitchen—when he'd been around. She also noticed the way her uncle looked at the young man every now and then. Seeing him now, clean-shaven, she didn't see how he'd reminded her uncle of her cousin.

"Where are you from, Mr. Ward?" she asked as they ate.

"Pittsburgh."

"And you worked in a stable or a livery there?"

His gaze met her uncle's. Mr. Ward looked down and leaned back in his chair. "No, I learned everything I know about horses from a man named Henry Farley. He trained racehorses."

Anne furrowed her brow. "Then you *did* work in a stable?"

"My family owned the stable."

Anne's eyes widened. She looked at her uncle.

"Mr. Ward is the poor relation of a rather wealthy family," her uncle explained.

"Oh," she said. "I see."

Mr. Ward glanced at her then returned to his dinner.

Anne frowned. He had to be hiding something. If he was trained to work with horses, why hadn't he found a job in a livery or a stable? Why tramp around—for who knows how many months—then become a janitor? Just because the charges for the fire had been dropped didn't mean he wasn't a wanted man elsewhere. She glanced at him, wondering if her uncle was letting his fatherly feelings for this young man lead him astray. His handsome face and charming manners might be hiding a more vicious nature than they imagined.

This thought drove Anne out to the stable the next morning. All sorts of scenarios had run through her head the night before—from Mr. Ward harming Scioto to out-and-out making off with him. She was relieved to see the horse's familiar face greet her when she came into the stable. He nudged and snuffed at her, clearly looking for food. Anne looked at his feed bin. It was empty. He hadn't been fed yet? Furious, she filled a bucket with oats and was about to open his stall door to pour it in when a sharp voice brought her to a halt.

"Stop!"

Anne whirled around to find Mr. Ward walking in the door with an old, banged-up pot, steam rising from its contents.

"If you don't mind," he said, looking from her to the stall door.

Anne opened it, and he poured the pot's contents into Scioto's bin. The horse sniffed it then began to eat with relish. Mr. Ward smiled and patted the horse on the neck.

"There you are, old man," he said. "Sorry, it took a little longer than I thought." He looked at Anne. "And I'm sorry if I sounded a bit rough. This is better for him than that."

Anne frowned. "Since when are oats poor feed for horses, Mr. Ward?"

"Oats are excellent for horses, but they're even better when they've been cooked."

"You cooked porridge for my uncle's horse?"

"Mrs. Werner gave me the same look." He laughed. "The German military cook their horses' feed. It helps them digest it."

"I've lived on a farm all my life, Mr. Ward. I've never heard of anything so outlandish."

"I assure you it works. My friend Henry Farley swears by it. I'll ease him onto it, of course, but he certainly seems to like it."

Anne frowned as she glanced at Scioto who, she had to admit, was enjoying his breakfast more than he usually did. The horse nudged Mr. Ward's arm. "You should feel honored. He doesn't take to new people so easily."

Mr. Ward's eyes locked on to hers. "I know. I guess he knows I'm someone he can trust."

Anne felt her face grow warm and she looked down.

"I have a deep regard for your uncle, Miss Kirby. He helped lead me to my faith in God. I can see how much Scioto means to him. And to you. I would never do anything to hurt him."

Anne reached over and stroked the horse's neck. The fact of the matter was, she really wanted to find something wrong with Peter Ward so she could still take care of Scioto. But her uncle had always been a good judge of character, and she couldn't ignore the sincerity in Mr. Ward's voice and face. *You'll be leaving soon.*

Maybe it's for the best. Feeling a hand on her arm, she jumped. Mr. Ward was looking at her curiously.

"Are you all right, Miss Kirby?"

"Yes, of course," she replied with a smile she knew had to looked forced. "He's finished eating. He likes to be groomed now."

Mr. Ward raised a brow at her but walked over to the tack room to fetch the grooming bucket. "I have to admit I'm almost sorry to be taking your job away from you," he said when he returned. "You did an excellent job."

Admiration shone in his green eyes, and her heart jumped in her chest. He was not quite as tall as her uncle, but he was close. Less than a head shorter, she estimated. And undeniably handsome. She decided he was indeed a dangerous man. Just not in the way she originally thought. "Thank you, but if you'll excuse me, I don't want to be late for work."

"You can come and visit him whenever you like."

She paused but didn't look back. "Thank you, Mr. Ward."

Peter stopped the buggy outside the stable and opened the wide door to the carriage stall. He turned. Dr. Kirby had already climbed down and now stood at Scioto's head, ready to lead him in.

"Here, sir, let me do that. It's what you pay me for," Peter said.

"Yes, so I do." Dr. Kirby chuckled as he moved to let Peter take him.

"Thank you for letting me come along with you to Professor Townshend's home for Thanksgiving dinner," he said, unhitching the horse. "I've never had a better one."

"Mrs. Townshend and her cook did themselves proud, didn't they?" he said. Peter released Scioto's harness from the shafts, and Dr. Kirby took hold of his bridle. "Here, allow me."

Peter pulled the buggy into its place then took Scioto and began unbuckling the harness. Scioto shook his head.

"You're ready for a rub down, aren't you, old man?" He smiled as the horse raised his head higher and pricked his ears forward.

Dr. Kirby laughed. "You're doing a fine job with him, Peter."

"Thank you, sir."

"Come in as soon as you're done. With Mrs. Werner visiting her family today, I'm afraid it will be up to me to make us some coffee."

Before long, Peter sat next to the professor in the parlor with a cup of the brew in his hands. It had turned quite chilly, and between the coffee and the fire dancing in the hearth, Peter soon felt quite warm.

"I'm surprised you didn't go with your niece to Ostrander, sir. I'm sure your family would have liked to see you."

"I'll see them at Christmas," Dr. Kirby said. "They're all coming down to visit with me then, and this big house will feel livelier for a change. The university originally built this for a professor with a much larger family, but he decided to teach elsewhere." He looked at Peter. "Will you be going back to Pittsburgh over Christmas?"

Peter squirmed. The professor was fishing for information again. For the past week, he'd been dropping hints and asking leading questions, attempting to encourage Peter to tell him more about his past. After leaving the courthouse, the professor had brought him here and demanded to know how he knew so much about horses. Peter told him about working with Henry and then told him he was a rich family's "poor relation." He'd hoped that would be enough to satisfy his curiosity, but the professor seemed determined to know more detail. Peter was at a loss to understand why. He chose his words carefully. "My family would probably rather I stay away."

"Oh?" The professor's eyes gleamed curiously.

"I didn't leave under the best of circumstances."

"I see." Expectant silence ruled for more than several moments. The professor finally broke it. "You're not going to tell me more, are you?"

"No, sir." He knew he should be able to trust Dr. Kirby with his past, but he still couldn't bring himself to tell him everything. Peter saw a frown form on his face, and he settled for a portion of the truth. "We had something of a falling out."

The professor studied him. "Does it have something to do with what you said in the courtroom? 'I haven't always been the man I am now.' I believe that's how you phrased it."

Peter stared into his coffee cup. "There are things in my past I'm not proud of, sir. I'd rather just leave it at that."

"I wish you would tell me, Peter."

"And I wish you would tell me why you were so adamant I work for you instead of helping me find a job at a stable in Columbus. Or why you insisted I shave my beard." He bit his lip, ashamed at himself for being so sharp. The fire snapped and crackled in the hearth. Peter looked up. But instead of a frown, the professor wore a strange kind of smile.

"You remind me of someone." He leaned back in his chair. "Has my niece been trying to help you in the stable?"

"No sir, she hasn't," he replied, surprised, yet relieved at the abrupt change in subject. "As a matter of fact, I only see her on mornings you both come to visit Scioto." That fact was a great relief to Peter. The knowledge that Anne Kirby was a very capable horsewoman made her even more attractive. The care she'd given Scioto had been excellent. She was like the jewel of great worth he'd read about in the Bible a few nights ago. A man would do just about anything to possess someone like her. *Stop it*, he told himself. *She's been hurt enough without the likes of you toying with her heart.*

"She wasn't happy to have you come along and replace her," the professor said thoughtfully. "But I promised her pa to keep her out of the stable. He and her ma want her to settle down and find someone to marry. She can't do that, doing men's work."

Peter sighed inwardly at the irony of the situation. The one person who wouldn't mind having a wife capable and willing to do man's work was the one person who didn't deserve her. *I'll only end up hurting her like all the others. Something about her will make me abandon her, and I just won't do that again, es-*

pecially to her. "I'll make sure she only comes to the stable to give Scioto the occasional sugar cube, sir," he said firmly.

But the morning after Anne's return, Peter came down to the stable to find Scioto had been groomed. His brow furrowed as he ran his hand over the horse's gleaming coat. There was no doubt she had done it, but *when*? Peter rose early to cook Scioto's feed before Mrs. Werner needed the stove for breakfast. Was it possible Miss Kirby had risen even earlier than that? He watched her carefully as they sat down to breakfast. She didn't appear tired. But something told him the cheerful face she put on was forced.

"Did you and Mr. Ward enjoy yourselves at Dr. Townshend's, Uncle?" she asked.

"Yes, our feast was very good. I don't have to ask about yours. Your ma is one of the finest cooks in all of Delaware County," he replied. "How is everyone? How is Millie getting on with that young man she's been seeing?"

Peter swore he saw all color leave Miss Kirby's face. The professor was taking a bite of his eggs and didn't notice. By the time he looked up again, she had pasted a smile on her face.

"Andrew Campbell proposed to Millie," she said, a little too brightly. "They want to get married in the spring."

"That's wonderful news!" the professor said. "I'll have to write to Jonah and congratulate them."

"Congratulations, Miss Kirby," Peter said. "I'm happy for your sister."

Anne nodded and picked up her plate as she rose from her place. "I am, too. Thank you, Mr. Ward."

He watched her walk into the kitchen, wondering just how happy she was. As it turned out, he didn't have to wait long to find out. After finding Scioto groomed for the next two mornings, he decided to confront her about it. He'd be breaking his promise to the professor if he didn't. He went to bed early and managed to wake up while it was still quite dark. He dressed quietly and saw a light as he crept downstairs from his room. She was standing in Scioto's stall, brushing him down. Something glinted on her face in the lamplight. He frowned. Was she crying?

"I love Millie, but I can't help but envy her happiness."

She spoke softly to the horse, but the tightness in her voice told him everything. He walked to the stall. The door stood open. He moved in behind her and gently laid his hand on her shoulder. Without thinking, he used her Christian name. "Anne?"

Her head dropped. "I'm sorry, Uncle Daniel."

Peter cleared his voice uncomfortably.

She turned to look at him. Her eyes widened.

"Mr. Ward!"

She thrust the brush she held into his hand and left the stall. Scioto started and pawed his straw, forcing Peter to lay a comforting hand on his neck and speak a few soothing words to him. By the time he'd calmed the horse, she was gone.

Chapter 11

Two days later, Anne stepped onto the streetcar, paid the fare, and settled into a seat near the rear of the car. She'd watched Mrs. Werner leave on an earlier car, and her uncle had left on Scioto an hour or so ago. He'd told her he didn't expect to be back until dinner. The only other person to evade was Mr. Ward, and that had been easy enough to accomplish since he spent most of his time in the stable.

Heat rose in her cheeks as if she'd sat in front of the fire too long. She closed her eyes. It had been a foolish thing to do; sneaking out to the stable so early to be with Scioto. She should never have snuck out to groom him. Then Mr. Ward wouldn't have suspected anything. How much had he heard the other morning? Worse, would he tell her uncle? It hadn't appeared he had yet, but that didn't mean he wouldn't. If he did, she'd come up with some sort of explanation. The harder thing to face was that she certainly couldn't risk sneaking out again.

The car left the area around the university and the rail yards approached. The road sloped downward and entered a short tunnel. Many trains had to cross High Street to get to Union Station, making the tunnel a necessary evil. The filth created by the streetcar horses made the odor within quite strong, even for Anne's farm-raised nose. She raised a handkerchief to her face, and she and the other passengers took a great gulp of fresh air when the car resurfaced.

She kept track of the streets as they rolled by so she wouldn't miss her stop. Spring Street, Long Street, Gay Street, and then finally, Broad Street. Broad and High bustled with activity, even on a Saturday. She got off and stood on the northwest corner of the intersection, admiring the tall three- and five-story buildings. Her favorite was a castle-like building directly across Broad Street. It was the Huntington Bank, where her uncle did business. He said Mr. Huntington, the owner, was one of the friendliest men who ever lived. She was smiling over what Uncle Daniel had told her about the banker greeting customers as he sat whittling on the steps of his bank, when the Broad Street streetcar stopped in front of her. Sharply reminded of her errand, the smile slipped away, and she got on, once again taking a seat near the back.

She carefully adjusted her bonnet, making sure it hid her face as much as possible, and wrapped her cloak closer. She was glad they were so worn that no one would wonder too much that they were out of fashion. Most would merely assume they were all she had to wear to keep out the chill.

Within fifteen minutes, a wide, well-kept lawn came into view. The streetcar stopped and she alighted with shaky hands. Rubbery legs took her up a long path to an imposing Gothic brick building. It had a mansard roof with two large square towers on both ends. An arched cupola rose from the center. Many simpler brick buildings spread out behind it on either side. She'd heard it was one of the better institutions; that its founder had been good friends of social reformer Dorothea Dix, and its patients were well treated. But that hardly made her visit to the Columbus Asylum for the Insane pleasant.

As Anne stepped through the doors, the visitor's attendant greeted her.

"Good morning, miss," the young man said. "I see you've come for another visit."

"If he's up to it," Anne said quietly.

"Why don't you sign in, and we'll find out."

Anne did as she was asked, taking care to sign in under the name of Wells, and sat down on a bench to wait. Before long her name was called, and she was led to the institution's conservatory. She'd been told on her visit last month that it was a recent addition to the asylum. A donor had left a certain sum of money with the wish that it be used for the benefit of the patients. Plants from all around the country had been purchased, some even donated by the National Conservatory in Washington.

But their lush beauty was lost on Anne as she was led to a wrought-iron bench where a man sat, stone faced, with hair as ginger red as her own. He was comfortably dressed and his hair and beard neatly trimmed. A large male attendant stood just a few feet away, and she nodded to him as she knelt down in front of the man. She swallowed in an effort to free the words that were sticking in her throat.

"Hello, Pa. I'm back to see you."

He said nothing. His brown eyes stared right through her, just as they had before. According to his doctor, whom Anne spoke with on her first visit, he hadn't always been completely motionless. In the years following the incident which led the Kirbys to adopt her, he had spoken wildly and at times had to be restrained. But over the last few months, he had slipped into this state. His attendant could move him in any position, and he remained that way. He either couldn't or wouldn't speak. Neither could he walk. His attendant had to carry him. Anne slowly sat next to him on the bench. She removed her bonnet and reached out to take one of his hands, which rested on his knees. It was cold and waxy, and his fingers refused to curl around hers.

She sat with him for some time, looking at him occasionally, willing him to return her gaze. He never did. Her emotions swung erratically, and she couldn't figure out which to lock on to—anger at what he had done or pity over what had happened to him. A great surge of shame and grief welled up inside her, threatening to burst forth like a flash flood during a spring thunderstorm. She managed to swallow most of it, but a stray tear escaped and splashed onto her free hand. Someone knelt at her feet and offered her a handkerchief. She looked up to find herself gazing into green eyes that were as filled with compassion as much as her own were filled with tears.

Anne took the handkerchief and used it to cover her face. She heard her father's attendant move forward.

"I should take him back to his room now, Miss Wells," he said.

She felt her father's hand slip from hers as his attendant picked him up to take him back to his room. As the footsteps faded away, Mr. Ward took the place beside her. He didn't speak, but Anne could feel the questions he wanted to ask. Who was that man? Why was she here? Why had the attendant called her Miss Wells? She took a shaky breath.

"That man's name is Robert Wells. He's my father. He lost his senses fighting the war…that's why the Kirbys adopted me. They never told me." She tried to go on, but months of pent-up emotion suddenly spilled out and she found herself leaning against Mr. Ward's shoulder, sobbing uncontrollably. She was dimly aware of his arm coming around her shoulders and pulling her close.

How long they sat there that way she didn't know. Her tears lessened, and he pulled her to her feet. He handed her the bonnet and, with wooden fingers, she put it on. He took her gently by the elbow and walked her out to the streetcar. Before she knew it, they were home. Mr. Ward walked her up to the door and she looked at him, apprehensively. What would he do now? Would he tell her uncle where she'd been?

"Get some rest, Miss Kirby," he said. "We'll talk later."

She went up to her room and lay down on her bed,

but rest was the last thing on her mind. Just what was Peter Ward planning to do?

Peter ran his hand down Scioto's leg. It still looked sound, and he smiled at the professor. "He's fine. It's healed nicely."

The professor smiled. "Good, then I must have been imagining things. I swore he started to limp a little."

They were outside the stable, the professor having just returned. Miss Kirby had joined them and looked on. Peter handed the bridle to her.

"Would you mind walking him around for me? I want to be sure he's sound."

He saw the questioning look in her eyes but didn't react to it. Pursing her lips, she took the reins from him and did as he'd asked. Peter watched them both as she walked Scioto back and forth. He'd hoped she would get some rest, but looking at her now, she still seemed troubled. When he had gone to the asylum today to visit Uncle Billy, he'd never dreamed he'd find her there. He was relieved that her problem was not what he'd originally imagined, but that didn't make it any less delicate. It was clear she was shouldering this burden by herself. As much as he was trying to keep her at a distance, she clearly needed to talk to someone, a person and not a horse. A thought occurred to him just as the professor's voice invaded his thoughts.

"Peter?"

He blinked. "Yes, sir?"

"I said he seems fine to me."

"Yes sir, he is." He smiled apologetically as he took

Scioto from Miss Kirby. "I'm sorry. I was a little lost in thought."

"What about?"

"Your niece." They both stared at him and he quickly rephrased his answer. "I meant I was wondering if I might trouble your niece to help me with something."

Miss Kirby arched an eyebrow at him then looked at her uncle. "What can I do for you, Mr. Ward?"

"As you know, I like to cook Scioto's feed in the morning and evening. But that takes time. Would it be possible for you to cook it and bring it out to me?"

She pursed her lips. "I would if I could cook, Mr. Ward."

The professor chuckled at Peter's surprised look. "Sad to say, it's true, in spite of my sister-in-law's best efforts."

"Well, I'm willing to give it *my* best effort." Peter smiled at Miss Kirby's doubtful look. "It's not hard, I promise. I'll be happy to show you after dinner if, of course, this is agreeable to you, Dr. Kirby."

"I don't see the harm in it." The professor smiled at his niece, who still seemed hesitant. "Go on and try. It can't hurt."

A few hours later, the two of them stood over the stove in Mrs. Werner's sparkling kitchen. Dr. Kirby, wishing them well, went into the library to grade papers. Miss Kirby looked around her with pursed lips. "I hope you're prepared to scrub this place down once we're finished, Mr. Ward."

Peter gave her a droll look and peeked into his worn

cook pot. "We're just boiling water right now, Miss Kirby."

She shook her head. "You haven't seen me in action."

"Here," he said, bringing forth a bucket of oats. "Put about two scoops of this into the water." She did so, and he handed her a flat wooden paddle. "Keep stirring it, so it won't scorch."

"Is this all we put in?"

"We need to add equal parts of wheat bran and salt, but not quite yet."

While she did spill some of the bran and the result was slightly scorched, Scioto didn't seem to notice. He munched away unconcerned, and a small smile graced Miss Kirby's face.

"You seem to be feeling better now."

The smile disappeared, and he instantly regretted his words. Her face was so much more beautiful when she smiled. "I hope we can forget about what happened earlier today, Mr. Ward. Thank you for your kindness in seeing me home, but it's really no longer your concern."

"I'm afraid I can't do that, Miss Kirby."

"Why?" Her brown eyes grew dark.

"No one should have to carry such a burden alone."

"I'm not carrying it alone," she retorted. She reached out and stroked Scioto's neck.

"As much regard as I have for Scioto, he's not going to answer you, and he's not going to help you solve anything."

"I don't need him to solve anything. I just need him to listen."

"That doesn't seem to be working out very well." He grasped her elbow, forcing her to face him. Her eyes were dark pools, glimmering in the lamplight. "It isn't, is it?"

"No," she whispered, and lowered her head against his chest.

Peter couldn't help but allow himself to wrap his arms around her. When he had asked God to send her someone who could help her, he hadn't imagined that He intended on sending him. *I don't want to hurt her, Lord. I don't trust myself not to.*

"Then trust Me."

Steeling himself, he gently pulled her away and led her over to a small bench across from Scioto's stall, near the harness room. He offered her his handkerchief. She took it with a small humorless laugh.

"I still have your other one."

"It's all right. I have plenty." He patiently waited for her to dry her face before speaking again. "Tell me about him."

Chapter 12

Anne looked at him for a long moment. He returned her gaze, his eyes filled with the same compassion he'd shown her as she sat beside her father at the asylum. Where was the fear, the revulsion? *He doesn't know all of it yet.* No, he didn't know everything. He might understand her natural father losing his senses, but he'd never understand the rest. She'd just have to be careful.

"I only found out about him a few months ago," she said. "The Kirbys had always told me I was adopted but never told me about him."

"To protect you," he stated.

Anne nodded.

"How did you find out?"

She shut her eyes against the memory. It had been a warm spring day, and Pa had sent her to find a letter from Uncle Daniel.

"Pa asked me to fetch a letter from the desk in the

parlor. I thought I found it, and when I opened it to be certain, I found a letter from…the asylum." The words she'd read still haunted her. *Mr. Wells's condition has not improved…He still has no knowledge that you and your wife adopted his daughter, Anne.* How she managed to find the right letter and give it to Pa with any measure of composure, she didn't know. "The asylum sends yearly updates to Pa through my uncle. I found most of them." Afterward, she'd slipped downstairs every night, piecing together the whole story.

"What about your natural mother? Did you find out what happened to her?"

Anne looked down, lest something in her expression tell him more than she wanted. "She died."

"Have you been praying about this?"

"I did at first. But the more I prayed, the more I realized—" She stopped, acutely aware that she'd almost revealed too much.

"Anne?" At the sound of her uncle's approach, relief seared through her, until she saw the expression on Mr. Ward's face. "Please don't tell him."

"He should know."

"No, please. He'll tell my parents and I don't want them to get hurt."

He hesitated then nodded reluctantly. "But you know you can't keep this from them forever."

"I know, and I won't; I promise." It was the truth. She'd always intended to tell her family, but only after she and her father were safely out West—when what he was and what he'd done couldn't threaten their reputation any longer.

* * *

A clear, cold December day had given way to a fiery purple dusk as Anne made her way to the stable with Scioto's feed. She'd been fixing it for two weeks now and when she delivered it in the evenings, she always lingered in the stable, watching Scioto eat and afterward, talking with Peter as he groomed him. She smiled as she knocked her foot against the door. When had they started calling each other by their Christian names? She couldn't be sure, but she knew because of their talks, her heart felt lighter than it had in months. It didn't make her departure any easier, but it didn't hang over her head like it had been. The door to the stable opened and she came face-to-face with Peter's devilish grin.

"What took you so long?"

Anne smiled reprovingly as she walked in. "I'm right on time as always."

"Of course you are." He shut the door. "I could set my watch by you." He lifted the latch that secured the top half of the stable door and pushed it open, as always. It made the stable a little chilly, but at least no one could accuse them of impropriety. Mrs. Werner had a clear view of them from the kitchen window.

"Here, let me take that from you." He poured the feed into Scioto's tub and set the pot down near the door for Anne to take with her when she went back inside. He leaned against the stable door next to her as they watched Scioto eat. "How's life in the library?"

Anne rolled her eyes. "Suffocating, literally."

"What do you mean?"

"When the Main Building isn't one big block of ice,

it stinks of sulfur fumes. Our new janitor can't seem to get the gas to work right."

Peter shook his head. "Mike tried to warn the board Mr. Pryce wasn't the man for the job."

"Well, it goes without saying that everyone misses you and Mike. I wish someone would help the poor man."

"Maybe I should go see him tomorrow after I have Scioto settled."

"Are you sure you should do that?" Peter had told her about his run-ins with the man. She didn't like the idea of him possibly being goaded into a fight.

"I might be able to help him. It's the right thing to do." Scioto finished eating, and Peter fetched the grooming kit from the tack room. Anne watched him in silence for a few minutes.

"Peter, what happened that made you become a tramp?"

His back was to her, but she could tell the question bothered him as his brush strokes slowed. In all their conversations, he'd never really brought up his past. He'd told her a few stories about working with Mr. Farley, but never anything about his childhood or who had raised him.

"Necessity," he replied.

"Did your family fire you? Or sell the stable?"

"The stable was sold."

"Then why didn't you get a job at another stable? I don't understand why your family would let you go homeless."

Peter turned and came over to the stall door. He looked gravely into her eyes. "Anne, my family and I had a falling out. I wasn't the best of men before I came here, and there are things in my past I'm not proud of. But I'm different now—a new creation, thanks to God—and I just want to leave all that behind me."

Anne nodded. She certainly understood what he meant about being ashamed of things in his past. Her eyes flicked to the stable floor. Her natural father had certainly given her nothing to be proud of. Peter ducked his head, catching her eye. She raised them, and he cocked his head at her. "Are you all right?"

She smiled slightly. "Yes, I'm fine."

He studied her face. "You're sure?"

She nodded.

"All right." He squeezed her hand then turned to continue grooming Scioto.

Anne was glad his back was to her again, so he wouldn't see the effect his touch had on her. Heat flew to her cheeks and a delicious thrill flowed from her head to her toes. She bit her lip as she tried to tamp it down. She had no business letting herself feel something for this man. This handsome, wonderful, faithful man who sometimes let her groom Scioto, when there was time before dinner, and who seemed to actually admire her ability with horses. He was everything she'd ever wanted in a man and more. She screwed her eyes shut. *Stop it.*

She would be gone in a few weeks. The school outside Topeka expected her, and the Topeka Insane Asylum had written to tell her they had room for her father. The letters were tucked in the waist of her skirt, beneath her bodice. She patted them to make sure they were still there. The only thing she had yet to do was speak to her father's doctor in Columbus. She wondered if Peter planned to go back to the asylum to visit the friend he'd told her about. The question was on the tip of her tongue when he spoke first.

"I enjoyed Reverend Aylsworth's lesson, yesterday." He smiled at her over the top of Scioto's back. Reverend Aylsworth was their pastor at Central Christian Church in Columbus.

"He preached on your favorite passage, didn't he? The 23rd Psalm." As hard as it had been to hear the sermon, she was glad Peter enjoyed it.

"It helped me keep my head together before I faced Mayor Walcutt." He finished grooming Scioto, unhooked the lead, and took off his halter. The horse nuzzled him and he rubbed his nose in return. He stepped out of the stall and paused in front of her. "I've been praying that for you."

"What?" She wished he'd tell her as he took the grooming bucket back to the tack room. It would be so much easier to breathe.

"That God would restore your soul. You still seem sad, sometimes, like you were a minute ago."

"I'm fine, Peter."

"Are you praying again?"

She nodded. She had started to pray again. Sort of. She prayed God would take away these feelings she had for him. If He didn't, leaving in a few weeks would be sheer torture.

"I'm glad." He didn't move, and Anne found herself getting lost in the green of his eyes. Mesmerized, she took a step closer to him. Just then, a nicker and a dark head appeared between them, and she all but cried out in relief.

"We should get inside. I'm sure Mrs. Werner has dinner ready," she said.

Peter shook himself, looking almost as relieved as she, and as she watched him walk to the tack room to put away the grooming bucket, she couldn't help wondering why. Was it because he also felt something? Or because he didn't?

"I still don't believe I did it," Anne said. "I actually fried an egg!"

"And I actually ate it," Dr. Kirby remarked, grinning. "And I'm still breathing."

Peter grinned at the semi-withering look she sent her uncle as the three of them walked toward the Main Building. Since he'd wanted to help Harvey with the heat today, he'd gotten up extra early and beaten Anne to the kitchen. Once he fed and watered Scioto, he came in to find her disappointed that the chore was already done. To make up for it, he taught her how to fry an egg.

"I told you it wasn't that hard," he said. "If I can do it, anyone can."

"If *you* can?" Dr. Kirby mused.

Peter looked over Anne to the professor, expecting to see that curious look of his. Instead he was greeted by a knowing smile. Uncertain what to make of it, Peter gave him a half-grin and looked out at the new coat of snow.

"Looks like Christmas will be white if the weather holds," he said.

"Yes," Anne replied softly. He glanced down at her. She had that sad, wistful look on her face again, the same one he'd tried hard not to kiss away in the stable yesterday.

He returned his gaze to the snow-covered campus. *Thank You for letting Scioto interrupt, Lord.* A few seconds more and she'd have been in his arms. *You sent me to help her, not break her heart. I'll try to be more self-controlled.* But even as he prayed, he felt a disappointment he didn't quite understand. He pushed it away as they approached the Main Building.

"Well, Peter," the professor said. "I sincerely hope your time with Mr. Pryce will be fruitful."

"Thank you, sir. I hope your day goes well, too."

"Oh it will, my boy, it will." He looked almost gleeful.

Anne noticed it as well and gave him a quizzical look as he kissed her cheek. "Are you feeling all right, Uncle Daniel?"

"The difficulties with the heat have given me the beginnings of a cold, I'm afraid," he replied. Peter couldn't help but grin at the look of consternation on Anne's face. That hadn't been the answer she was looking for. Dr. Kirby either didn't notice or pretended not to as he went on. "Are you coming up with me?"

"I think I'll wait for Emma. She should be along any moment," she replied slowly.

"Tell her I said 'hello' then," Dr. Kirby said. Nodding to Peter, he turned and walked up the stairs and went inside.

"I'm glad to see him so happy," Anne said as she and Peter looked after him. "I just can't imagine why he is."

"He's up to something," he said.

"How do you know?"

"My granddad used to get the same look in his eye. It always meant—" He stopped himself as he realized what he'd just said. He hazarded a look at Anne. Despite that they weren't related by blood, Peter couldn't help noticing she and Dr. Kirby had similar expressions of curiosity.

He sighed. "All right, you caught me. My grandfather raised me after my mother died when I was a toddler."

"Oh, Peter, I'm so sorry. What happened to your father?"

"He abandoned my mother before I was born. I've never met him."

He was glad they were standing outside with students walking here and there on their way to class. The look of sympathy on her face was so endearing, he struggled not to embrace her.

"I haven't seen my uncle look that happy since before Aunt Kitty died," she said.

"Aunt Kitty? You mean his wife, Katherine?"

"Yes. That was my own special name for her. My brother and sister called her Aunt Katherine, but to me, she was always Aunt Kitty." The corners of her mouth curled thoughtfully. "It's because I always heard Uncle Daniel calling her Kat."

"I saw her picture on the mantel in the parlor," Peter said. "She seemed like a very kind and gracious lady."

"Oh she was." Anne's smile grew as she recalled her aunt. "I loved listening to her talk. She was from South Carolina."

"Really? Did your uncle meet her during the war?" Peter asked. He recalled the professor telling him he'd been a major in the Union army.

"No, she came north after the war ended. A lot of people didn't like that she was Southern, but Uncle Daniel didn't care. In spite of everything, he loved her anyway..." The sad look returned to her eyes.

Peter frowned. *She deserves to be happy*, he thought. *And I'd like nothing better than to spend the rest of my life making that her way.* His heart nearly stopped in shock. He stared at Anne, looking at her in a way he'd never looked at another woman. He plumbed the brown depths of her eyes, and Anne's cheeks, already crimson from the cold, became even more so, and she looked away.

"Good morning."

They both started. Emma Long stood before them.

"Good morning," Anne said, her voice breathless with relief. "Emma, do you remember Mr. Ward? He used to work for Mike."

Emma's eyes widened. "I thought I recognized you. You certainly look different without that beard!"

Peter tore his eyes away from Anne long enough to tip his hat. "Thank you, Miss Long." He looked back at Anne, who still avoided his gaze.

Emma locked arms with Anne, her eyes dancing. "We should get inside, it's nearly nine o'clock."

"Yes of course." Anne quickly glanced at him as she turned to leave. "Take care today. I'll see you later."

Peter nodded and watched as she and Miss Long

walked up the steps of the Main Building. His mind still whirled. He couldn't quite believe it. For the first time in his life, he found himself truly and deeply in love.

Chapter 13

"**Y**ou've come to gloat, haven't you?"

Harvey Pryce stood outside the boiler house, his arms crossed. Peter had stood what seemed like forever outside the building, waiting for him to show up. Pryce looked anything but happy to see him.

"Who sent you? Mr. Cope?"

"No one sent me. I heard about your problem and wanted to help."

"I don't need your help!"

"Harvey, we both know the buildings aren't being heated properly," Peter said. "Just tell me what's wrong."

The man still scowled at him. "It's the coal. It's not good quality."

"What happened? Did you stop buying from Lyonsdale Coal Company?"

"It's just bad coal is all."

"Let me come in and see what's going on."

"Why? You want your job back?"

"No, I have a new job now."

Harvey's expression softened. A little. "Oh yeah, thought I heard that. You work for Professor Kirby, don't you?" Peter nodded and a little more of the hardness fell from his face. "He's one of the few professors who's been decent to me about all this."

"He's a good man," Peter said.

"Was it him who's getting you to do this?"

"No, but it's his good example. He's the one who took me in after you gave me that timber lesson."

Harvey's shoulders dropped and his arms fell to his sides. "Why didn't you let Mayor Walcutt charge me?"

" 'Therefore if thine enemy hunger, feed him,' " Peter quoted. " 'If he thirst, give him drink.' "

" 'For in so doing thou shalt heap coals of fire on his head.' " Harvey finished the quote. "Don't look so surprised. My ma taught me that when I was young. Guess I kinda forgot a lot of things she taught me. If she could see me now, she'd sure heap coals of fire on my head."

Peter smiled and slapped him on the shoulder. "How about I help you heap coals of fire, so the university stays warm? I'll show you how it's done."

"Would you mind an awful lot helping me out today? Frank's sick."

"Sure."

It was nearly dark by the time they finished; but in the end, Peter had helped him get caught up in a number of things and made sure Harvey knew how to properly maintain the heat. Most important of all, Harvey promised he'd come to church. Peter offered to lend him his Bible, but the man declined, saying he had his mother's old one tucked away.

Judging from the sky, he knew Anne and Dr. Kirby had already headed for home and, more than likely, were already there. Despite how busy he'd been, Anne hadn't been far from his thoughts all day. He still marveled over how he felt about her. Shaking his head, he smiled. A Pittsburgh society matron, whose daughter he'd courted then dropped, once said the three rivers would turn purple before Peter McCord fell in love. The Monongahela, the Allegheny, and the Ohio rivers must be positively violet by now, because that day had finally come.

If he'd thought her beautiful the first time he'd seen her picture, she was more than twice that now. All the qualities a young lady needed to start a home—she didn't possess. By her own admission, she couldn't sew, could barely cook, and would rather spend her time in a stable than a parlor. By society's standards, she was a failure. But she was perfect as far as he was concerned—perfect for him.

Now he had to convince her it was possible for him to love her. The way she'd spoken about her aunt and uncle suggested she didn't feel worthy of someone's love. He smiled roguishly. No worries there. He had plenty of experience in that department. Best of all, he would mean every charming word he intended to utter. And for the rest of his life, every gallant deed would be exclusively reserved for Anne Kirby. He lifted his head to the dusky sky. *Thank You, Lord. I see now the path You want me to follow. Thank You for these green pastures and still waters.*

He was thankful when he arrived at the path between Professor Tuttle's and Professor Kirby's. It hadn't been a long walk, but it'd certainly been a cold one. In the failing light, he could just make out the stable. He frowned. The door gaped open. He began to jog until he heard a voice cry out. Certain that it was Anne's, he broke into a run, covering the distance in seconds. He skidded to a stop in the stable doorway. His heart dropped at the sight before him. Scioto lay thrashing on the floor of his stall. Anne, halter in hand, stood just inside the door, dodging his flailing hooves to reach his head.

Scioto grunted and let out a short squeal. As soon as she'd seen him down, Anne's only thought had been to get him back on his feet. Again, she attempted to get around his hooves, but a strong arm wrapped around her waist and yanked her back.

"No," she cried out. "He'll hurt himself."

As she was pulled out of the stall, she twisted herself around and came face-to-face with Peter. Silently, he took the halter from her and entered the stall. She started after him but found herself pulled backward into her uncle's arms.

Scioto squealed, and Anne gasped as his hoof flew dangerously close to Peter's head. Peter dodged it and moved nearer the horse's head. He slipped on the halter, and after several dreadful minutes, pulling and shouting, Peter managed to get Scioto on his feet. He immediately led the horse out of the stall before he could lie down again.

"I need to walk him," he said, his broad chest heaving like a bellows as the two left the stable. "Get the box stall ready."

Anne grabbed a pitchfork and began spreading straw. The box stall was larger than the other two stalls. Should Scioto begin to thrash again, he'd have more room to move. She winced at the thought. She turned. Her uncle had entered, sleeves rolled up and tie hanging loose around his neck. They finished quickly, and he looked at her. "What happened?"

"I came out to light the lamp and get feed to cook for him." Her voice shaking, Anne took a deep breath, trying to steady it. "When I didn't see him at the stall door, I looked in—" She couldn't go on, and her uncle pulled her close.

"Let's pray it's just a mild case of colic," he said.

Anne nodded against his chest. They both looked up as Peter returned with Scioto. Grabbing their pitchforks, they quickly moved out of the way as Peter led the horse into the stall. Anne's hand flew to her mouth in horror as she watched Scioto kick at his belly and roll his eyes, drenched in his own sweat. She'd seen colic in one of Pa's plow horses. But this was much, much worse. Peter struggled to keep him from lying down again. He glanced at her uncle.

"He needs a veterinarian, sir. This is beyond me."

Uncle Daniel nodded. "By God's grace, one just happens to be staying with Dr. Townshend." He grabbed his coat from where he'd thrown it on the stable floor. "I'll be back with him as soon as I can."

Anne gripped the post next to the door. Peter looked exhausted, his brown hair dampened with sweat despite the cool air. "Let me come in and help you."

"No! He's in too much pain and I won't have him hurting you." Scioto brushed against the wall. "I don't understand this. I checked on him at noon and he was fine."

"Colic can come on quick."

"But what caused it? We've been so careful about his feed and water."

Anne swallowed the lump in her throat. They'd been very careful with Scioto's care, but they both knew the reason for the condition could be something neither could help nor foresee. It was a fact that Anne felt Peter, at least for the moment, refused to accept.

"I need to walk him again," he said, pulling the poor horse through the door and outside once more.

Anne followed, hoping the movement would bring Scioto relief as was usual in a case of colic. But the more he moved, the more the agony increased, and Peter soon walked him back inside. Scioto shivered and slowly lowered himself to the stable floor. Peter sank down on his knees near Scioto's head.

"Let him rest," he said as Anne cautiously entered the stall. "He's exhausted and so am I."

She knelt down and laid her hand on Scioto's neck. He didn't respond to her touch. He simply lay there, his breathing labored. She turned her attention to Peter, who looked at the horse miserably, his eyes dark, the green in them barely showing.

"What did I do wrong?"

She took his hand, forgetting herself at the sight of the wretched look on his face.

"You didn't do anything wrong. You know this might be something neither of us could have stopped."

He groaned and pulled her closer, laying his head on her shoulder. Her heart beat furiously, but there was no way she could pull away, he was hurting too badly. Instead her traitorous hand stroked the damp ends of his hair. Scioto began to thrash, and Peter quickly hauled her up and outside the stall. He calmed again and lay still. Anne looked down at her fingers, entwined with Peter's. And they stood there that way, watching Scioto until her uncle returned. Professor Townshend accompanied him, along with another man. The man, with white hair, a long beard to match, and round spectacles, introduced himself as Dr. Henry Detmers. His German accent, while slightly thicker than Anne's mother's, sounded comforting and familiar. He immediately entered the stall, and Peter followed him.

"Did walking him help?" Dr. Detmers knelt down beside Scioto.

Peter shook his head. "It seemed to make him worse."

The doctor frowned and felt the horse's legs and ears. "Cold," he muttered, and Anne saw Peter's face harden, his mouth forming a thin line as the doctor's fingers pressed on Scioto's throatlatch, taking his pulse.

"It's red colic, isn't it?" Peter asked quietly.

"Enteritis, yes, I'm afraid so." Dr. Detmers opened his black satchel. "I won't attempt to check his belly. I can tell now it will only pain him. We'll need to administer linseed tea and laudanum." He looked up at Dr.

Townshend, standing next to Anne. "Unfortunately, I don't have as much of either with me as I would like."

"I have more at my home," Dr. Townshend replied.

"And I'll make the tea—as much as you need—" Anne offered.

Dr. Detmers continued treating Scioto far into the night, assisted by Peter. The medicine seemed to calm him, but in the end, they could only wait. Mrs. Werner made coffee, which Anne tirelessly took to the men several times over the course of the night. When she came out with yet another serving, Peter looked at her wearily.

"You should go to bed," he said as she set the tray down on a small table they'd brought down from Peter's room.

"I want to stay," she replied as she poured a cup.

Uncle Daniel joined them at the table. "Anne, it would be best if you went inside."

She shook her head and handing him the cup, found he already held something in his hand. His Colt, the one he'd used during the war. She dropped the cup and grabbed his arm.

"Uncle Daniel, no, he might get better." She felt Peter gently grip her shoulders.

"Anne," he said close to her ear. "It's been hours now. There's no change and he's suffering."

Tears sprang to her eyes as she laid her hand over her mouth, allowing the truth of his words to sink into her heart. *Oh Lord, is there truly nothing else to be done?* She bowed her head at the answer. Her uncle took her hand and squeezed it. He looked wretched, having spent most of the night pacing back and forth outside the stall. Disheveled hair and bloodshot eyes, he had the look of a man who'd been keeping vigil, as he had the horrible night Aunt Kitty slipped away. As much as it hurt, she knew it was best for Scioto.

He flicked his eyes from hers to Peter's. "Take her inside."

"Sir," he said, his voice rough. "This is my fault, I should—"

"No, Peter. You're not for one second to believe that. You've taken better care of this horse than even I did when he first came to me. This happened for reasons known only to God. I've accepted that."

As he spoke, Scioto groaned. They approached the stall, and Anne watched as he struggled for a few moments then lay very still. Dr. Detmers felt for his pulse and shook his head. Scioto was gone.

Anne buried her face in her hands. Peter wrapped his arm around her waist, pulling her close, and she felt the warmth from his brow resting on the back of her head. Quiet filled the stable; the only sound was that of Dr. Detmers putting away his instruments. Taking a deep breath, Anne lifted her head. Peter released her as Dr. Townshend offered his handkerchief. Taking it, she gave him a watery smile. "Thank you for staying, Dr. Townshend."

"You're very welcome, my dear." He looked at Uncle Daniel. "Some students and I will come and get him tomorrow."

"Thank you, Norton." He offered his hand to Dr. Detmers. "Thank you for coming on such short notice."

Dr. Detmers shook it. "You're welcome, Dr. Kirby." His eyes swept over to Peter. "You were a great help to me tonight, young man. You should consider becoming a veterinary surgeon yourself."

Peter smiled thinly. "I'm afraid I never was much for book learning, sir, but thank you."

Even as tired as she was, his comment piqued Anne's curiosity. Was this yet another clue to Peter's past? She chastised herself. *It doesn't matter now. You'll be going away soon.* She realized, startled, that Peter actually would go away before her. With Scioto gone, he had no job and no reason to stay. The thought should've brought her relief. Instead, it hurt her so keenly she reached out her hand to steady herself. Her uncle grasped it and her elbow, and she leaned against him.

"It's time you went to bed," he said firmly.

"And sleep yourself out," Dr. Townshend said. "Make sure she stays home tomorrow, Daniel."

"I can't. Emma needs me at the library," Anne protested. But everything finally began to take its toll on her, and she found she could no longer keep her eyes open. Before she knew what happened, her uncle helped her inside and Mrs. Werner tucked her into bed.

Chapter 14

Peter began straightening up the stable. He'd slept all day yesterday, only waking when Dr. Townshend and some students came to haul away Scioto's body. After that, he slept fitfully and came down early this morning to work. He mucked out the stalls, and then laid down fresh straw in each one. He checked the harnesses and bridles, oiled Dr. Kirby's saddle, and looked over the buggy three times. When he finished, he stepped back, frowning. Why on earth was he doing all this—for a horse that was no longer here?

As he worked, he'd gone over everything he'd done those last hours of Scioto's life. Nothing had been amiss, *nothing*. The horse had been right as rain when he fed and watered him that morning. And when he'd come home at noon, Scioto had pranced around the paddock without a care in the world. He looked at the rag in his hand and threw it on the ground. *What was it, Lord? What did I do to kill him?*

"It wasn't your fault, Peter."

He turned. Dr. Kirby stood in the door of the stable. He closed it behind him, walked over, and laid a fatherly hand on his back. "There was nothing you could have done."

"There had to be *something*!"

He squeezed his shoulder. "No, Peter. Dr. Detmers and Dr. Townshend performed a necropsy this morning. He twisted his intestine somehow. It had nothing to do with your care of him. Not even your friend Henry Farley could have prevented it." Peter looked at him. The professor's face was sad but firm. "I won't have you beating yourself up over this. Let him go."

He nodded, weighing Dr. Kirby's words. How many times had Henry told him about the possibility of something like this happening to a horse? And burying himself with guilt wouldn't help anyone. "Yes, sir," he said finally.

"We must be 'forgetting those things which are behind, and reaching forth unto those things which are before.'" He looked over at Scioto's empty stall. "Not that any of us will be forgetting him anytime soon."

"No, sir," Peter replied. It would be a long time before he forgot Scioto, if ever. He took a deep breath. "I guess I better pack my things."

Dr. Kirby looked at him sharply. "What are you talking about?"

"What would you have me do, sir? I can't stay here and do nothing all day."

"I'll find something for you to do," the professor snapped.

Peter's eyes widened. He hadn't meant to make him angry. Dr. Kirby's brow smoothed, and he patted him on the back.

"Please, stay. I'll get a new horse in time. And you must stay for Christmas. The rest of the family is eager to meet you."

"All right," he said slowly. "Although, I can't imagine why you would tell your family anything about me."

"Why shouldn't I?" he asked. "Anne's brother, Jacob, is eager to speak with you. He's been thinking of raising Percherons for profit."

Peter didn't hear the rest of what Dr. Kirby said. His mention of Anne had drowned out all else. "Sir, if you don't mind my asking, how is your niece?"

The professor regarded him carefully, and Peter looked away. In spite of everything that occurred that night, Dr. Kirby clearly noticed the way he had embraced Anne after Scioto passed. But he didn't mention it when he spoke.

"She slept late into the day yesterday," he said. "And claims to have slept fine last night." The concern in his eyes told Peter she hadn't looked it. "She's very insistent that we allow her to go to the library today."

"You should let her, sir. It will take her mind off everything."

"You're probably right." A small smile spread over the professor's face. "You two are getting along very well."

Peter felt his face redden and, looking down, rubbed the back of his neck.

"Anne's adopted, you know."

He looked up, surprised. "Yes, sir, I know. She told me."

Dr. Kirby's smile broadened like that of a Cheshire cat's. "Did she? I'm glad." Before Peter could say anything else, he went on. "It's time for us to leave. Mrs. Werner mentioned some repairs you might do around the house." He gave Peter a final pat on the back and left.

He would've put more thought into what Dr. Kirby said if he hadn't missed Anne so much all that day. She was never far from his thoughts, and he sent many prayers up for her as he helped Mrs. Werner around the house. The professor's family would be arriving in a week, on Christmas Eve, and he helped her lift things down from closets and made minor repairs here and there. They finished not long before Anne and Dr. Kirby were due home, and Peter went out to the stable. He changed into clean clothes then walked downstairs. There was Anne, standing in front of Scioto's stable.

She heard him and turned. His heart nearly broke at the sight of her face. Her eyes looked dull and dark. Circles stained the fair skin beneath them. She certainly hadn't slept well last night. Even her fiery, ginger hair seemed less brilliant. He walked closer. His arms ached to hold her. Instead, he gripped the stall door while she directed her gaze to the lonely bed of straw within.

"I still can't believe he's gone," she said.

"Neither can I."

"He was the first horse I ever rode," she whispered. "I was five. I was visiting Uncle Daniel and Aunt Kitty. Uncle Daniel had ridden Scioto to a meeting and when I saw them trotting up, I ran out to meet them. He asked me if I wanted to ride Scioto. He was such a big horse that I was a little frightened. But Uncle Daniel said Scioto would take care of me." She looked at him, her eyes bright, filling with tears. "And he did. He knew— as soon as Uncle Daniel put me in the saddle—he went so slow, so steady."

Her voice broke on the last word, and Peter couldn't stand it any longer. He pulled her into his arms and allowed the waves of her grief to break against him, rubbing her back as she shook with sobs. When her tears were finally spent, she lifted her head but didn't look up at him.

"I've spoiled your shirt," she said, vainly wiping at it with her hand.

"I have another," he said, lifting her chin. Her eyes wandered hesitantly over his face. A few tears still shone on her cheeks, and he gently wiped them away with his thumb and forefinger. She swallowed and her eyes darted away, but he continued looking at her until they once again locked on to his. He leaned in and gently brushed her forehead with his lips, her curled bangs brushing his skin like a feather. He longed to kiss her but knew this wasn't the time for it. He wouldn't take advantage of her grief. She stepped back and he released her.

"It's time we went in for dinner." Her voice was soft and shaky, and she wouldn't look at him.

"I'll be there in a minute."

She nodded and slipped out the door.

Chapter 15

The next week slipped away quickly, and Anne's grief at losing Scioto eased. A bittersweet pang rose in her heart whenever she thought about him, but she comforted herself with the knowledge his passing had not gone unnoticed by God.

" 'And one of them shall not fall on the ground without your Father,' " she whispered as she and Uncle Daniel walked home from the Main Building.

"Did you say something, my dear?"

"I was just thinking of Matthew 10:29."

He nodded. "Yes, that one has been on my thoughts as well."

"He was a good horse," she said, squeezing his arm.

"Peter said it's lonely in the stable without him."

Anne almost started at the sound of his name. That evening in the stable never seemed to be far from her thoughts. She'd felt so comforted in his arms, and she relished in remembering how tender his green eyes had been in the soft lamplight. The kiss he'd placed on her forehead made her dizzy just thinking about it. And over the past week, he'd been very attentive to her, pulling out her chair at dinner and drawing her into the conversations between him and her uncle while they sat together in the parlor. It was as if he were courting her. Her heart leapt as she realized it, and she fought for control. *Stop it! Uncle Daniel may have decided to keep him on, but* you're *still leaving.* She laid her hand at the side of her waist, feeling the crinkle of her letters tucked in her bodice, her resolve slipping. Maybe Peter was different. Unlike Sam, he'd seen her father firsthand, and it hadn't made a difference. Dare she tell him the rest? *No. I can't stray from this path. Besides, even if he understands I can't do that to him. I love him too much.* Her breath caught in her throat as she finally admitted her feelings for him to herself.

It caught again, later, when she came down to dinner and Peter smiled at her. He stood behind her chair, as usual, and as he helped her slide it beneath the table, she happened to look at her uncle. His eyes twinkled and a smile played at the corner of his mouth. She bit the inside of her lip. Wasn't everything hard enough already without knowing that her uncle approved of Peter's regard for her?

"I hope you both had a good day," Peter said. He spoke to both of them, but he was looking at her.

"It was fine," Anne said, averting her eyes to serve her uncle. "It's actually been rather boring, now that term examinations are coming to an end. No one needs the library for now."

"You mean, aside from the other times when it's not?" he asked slyly.

Anne couldn't help looking up and smiling. He knew, so well, how tedious she found her job. "In fact, Emma told me to take the day off tomorrow."

"Excellent," Uncle Daniel said. "That actually fits right in with my plans." He turned to Peter. "Dr. Townshend came to see you today?"

"He did."

"Everything is arranged, then?"

"Yes sir, everything's ready."

Anne looked at both of them quizzically. "What's going on?"

"Why Anne, I'm so glad you asked," her uncle said. Anne sighed. As if she could do anything but, what with the sly smiles on both their faces. Her uncle continued. "Peter wondered if you could help him with something tomorrow."

She knew it would be better to refuse, but her heart and her mouth turned traitor on her. "Of course, what is it?"

"A surprise." Peter's eyes shone as bright as a spring day. "I'll show you tomorrow, after we walk your uncle to the Main Building."

The next day, Anne's curiosity peaked as Peter led her away from the Main Building. Especially when he stopped after a few steps and looked at her.

"Do you trust me?"

The playful look in his eyes was so charming she almost forgot to answer. "Yes—of course," she stammered.

"Close your eyes."

Anne looked at him momentarily then obeyed. He took her hands in his. Despite that they both wore gloves, the warm pressure of his fingers sent slivers of delight coursing through her.

He gently guided her over snow-covered paths and across what she thought might be Neil Avenue, which ran through the university grounds. She wasn't familiar with this part of campus, and she couldn't imagine where he was taking her. They came to a stop.

"Now don't peek," Peter said.

He removed her glove and guided her hand. At the same time her fingers made contact with something warm, soft, and smooth, the wind changed direction and a familiar scent reached her nose. Her eyes flew open. A sweet bay mare stood before her, hitched to a fence outside the university farm buildings. Anne took in the horse's markings, eyes widening as she recognized her.

"This is Spice," she said. "She belongs to Dr. Townshend. He brought her to our farm this past summer to breed with Scioto. What's she doing here?" The reason quickly dawned on her, and her jaw dropped as she looked at Peter. "He's giving the foal to Uncle Daniel?"

Peter nodded. He took her hand and smiled. "That's not all. If you want her, Spice belongs to you."

Anne looked at the mare with mixed emotions. She'd liked Spice while she was at the farm over the summer. She was so gentle and sweet tempered, Anne had jokingly told Dr. Townshend she should've been named Sugar. Stroking her neck, she wondered how she'd feel seeing her in Scioto's stall when she remembered it didn't matter. She might as well say "yes," and leave a note for Uncle Daniel when she left, giving Spice to him. Not trusting her voice, she nodded.

Peter looked down at her. "Are you sure? I know it's soon—"

She swallowed hard. "Yes, it's fine. Besides, Uncle Daniel said he was going to get another horse soon. It might as well be one I'm familiar with."

His smile warmed her and, for the moment, chased away the rest of her tears. "Then let's get her home and settled in."

With Spice loping placidly along behind them, Anne remembered she hadn't had a chance to speak with him privately since that evening in the stable. Her heart began to pound and she yanked her focus to the question she had to raise.

"When do you plan to visit your friend Uncle Billy again?"

Peter looked down at her, his brows slightly furrowed. "Why do you ask?"

Anne chastised herself. She should've asked a less straightforward question. What had she been thinking? When she didn't answer, Peter's frown deepened, and she groped for an explanation. "I just wondered..." Her voice trailed off and she looked away.

"The doctors at the asylum found Billy's family in Indiana," he replied quietly. "They contacted them and sent him home."

"Were they able to help him?"

Peter brought Spice to a stop, forcing Anne to do so as well. She felt his gloved hand lift her chin and looked into his stern but gentle face.

"I know what you want to do," he said. "I don't mind taking you to see him. But I won't do it until you tell your uncle that you know. No more sneaking around."

She nodded. She'd have to write to her father's doctor then. But Peter's words had sent her determination wavering again like a leaf caught by the wind. He was willing to visit her father? He didn't mind? *Father, I'm so confused. What should I do?* The answer laid on her heart only confused her further. No, it wasn't possible.

She was still pondering it when they got back to the stable. Once they had Spice settled in her stall, Peter brought out the grooming bucket. He smiled at Anne and handed it to her. She took it and gazed at it reflectively. Would this be the last time she'd do this? Or not? She looked at Peter.

"What's wrong?"

"Nothing." She started to work but winced as she found how hard it was to groom Spice today. She usually wore a simple skirt and shirtwaist when she worked in the stable. But the dress she wore now draped around her front, its bustle brushing the sides of the stable. Not to mention the sleeves were quite snug. She glanced at Peter. "I'm afraid you'll have to do it. I'm not dressed for this."

He grinned at her. "You do look as if you stepped right out of a fashion plate." He took the brush. "But then you look lovely no matter what you wear."

It took a full minute for her to organize her thoughts again. Once they were set to rights, she watched Peter groom Spice. He had an easy smile on his face.

"You look content," she said.

"I am." He gave Spice's coat one more swipe with

a soft cloth, put it back in the bucket, and carried it out of the stall. He leaned against the doorframe. "I'm very happy with where the Lord ended up leading me."

Her brows rose at his wording. "Where He 'ended up' leading you?"

"When I first came to Columbus and gave my life to Christ, I thought God wanted me to be a true 'new creation,' leaving behind everything from my old life." He rubbed Spice's nose. "I didn't think He would lead me to work with horses again." His eyes locked on to hers. "And I never thought He'd lead me to you."

Everything in the world fell away as she lost herself in the passionate green of his eyes. He reached out, toying maddeningly with one of the ringlets at the base of her neck before stroking her cheek with the back of his thumb. Cupping her face in one hand, he wrapped his other around her waist and pulled her closer. A roguish grin gently played across his face before his lips finally found hers.

Nothing else existed except the soft warmth of his lips, the faint scent of shaving soap, and the gentle pressure of his hand on her waist. Everything she ever wanted was in this moment, and she didn't want it to end. She refused to open her eyes when he lifted his head. She clung to him, their foreheads still touching.

"Anne," he whispered.

This time she kissed him, her hands buried in his chocolate brown hair. Something prodded her at the back of her mind, something she should be remembering, something important. But the sweet forgetfulness of his kiss drove it far from her thoughts, until he finally raised his head again.

"Anne, I love you," he whispered in her ear. "Nothing else matters."

Sudden and painful remembrance gripped her heart and nearly stopped it. She backed away, her eyes rapidly filling with tears. Peter's face, full of shock and confusion, only added to her pain.

"I can't," she said. "I can't do this again. I'm sorry."

She turned and ran from the stable, not stopping until she'd reached her room.

Chapter 16

The words danced in front of Peter's eyes for the millionth time since he'd found the letters lying in the straw in Spice's stall.

The Topeka Insane Asylum will be happy to make room for your father, Robert Wells, at your earliest convenience. Please have his doctor at the Columbus Asylum for the Insane send us all necessary records....

He'd started after her then stopped himself. Mrs. Werner would wonder what was going on if she saw him chasing Anne from the barn to the house. He walked back inside and found Spice pawing at something and discovered two letters addressed to Anne Wells, care of the university library. He was more than willing to obey the nudge he felt God giving him to open them.

The first was the letter from the asylum. The other one, from some school district in Kansas, offered Anne a position teaching school as soon as she could make the arrangements. He shook his head at himself. Why hadn't he seen it? He knew that because of her father she didn't feel worthy of someone's love but hadn't imagined she'd take it this far. No wonder she wanted to go to the asylum again. She needed to talk to her father's doctor.

Peter rose from the bench near the harness room and ran his hands through his hair. He had to tell Dr. Kirby. He had no choice. She'd be angry, that was certain, but she'd get over it. There was no way on earth he was going to let her do this.

The stable door opened and Dr. Kirby walked in. He smiled at Peter, but it quickly faded.

"What is it?" Dr. Kirby looked toward Spice, who dozed in her stall. "Where's Anne?"

Saying nothing, Peter handed the professor the letters he'd found.

The more the professor read, the graver his face became. He looked at Peter. "You knew about this?"

"About her natural father, yes, but I had no idea she was making plans to take him and head out West." He explained how Anne had found out about her father. "Why does she feel the need to leave? I know most people can be unkind about things like this but—" He stopped at the look on Dr. Kirby's face. "What is it?"

Dr. Kirby motioned him toward the bench. "You should probably sit down, son."

* * *

On Christmas Eve, Peter stood at the mirror in the professor's room, tying one of his famous four-in-hand knots. When he finished, he stepped back and looked at himself. He hadn't worn such fine clothes in—had it really been only months? It felt like years. He shrugged into the frock coat he'd borrowed from the professor and turned to face him. The professor stood just behind him, a small smile on his face.

"You know this is ridiculous, don't you? It's never going to work."

"Yes it will," the professor said, adjusting his own tie. He pulled at his vest to smooth out nonexistent wrinkles and brushed at his coat. "We should get downstairs. My family will be arriving soon."

Peter sighed and followed him down the stairs. He shouldn't have let the professor talk him into this. He certainly had a better understanding now of just why Anne felt she had to leave, but the solution Dr. Kirby had suggested—*Having me propose to her? In front of her family? Wouldn't telling her pa make more sense?*

They reached the bottom of the stairs and walked into the parlor. A yet-undecorated Christmas tree stood in the corner near the front window, and bunches of holly and fir bows lined the mantel. But Peter's eyes noticed only Anne, who stood in front of the tree.

Despite that it was Christmas Eve, when he saw her, all he could think of was autumn. With her deep green dress, red hair, and doe-brown eyes, she looked like fall in all its magnificent glory. He'd never seen her so beautiful, yet the picture was marred by the way she looked at the tree. She had that sad, wistful look in her eyes again, and if it hadn't been for the professor adjusting the logs in the fire, he would've yanked her into his arms and kissed her until that look vanished. He walked over to her, hands clasped tightly behind him.

"Your uncle tells me your parents are bringing more decorations," he said. He'd helped Mrs. Werner bring down Dr. Kirby's small crate of decorations the other day. It sat on the floor next to the tree.

She turned to him, her eyes widening. There was no mistaking the admiring look in them as she took in his appearance, but she quickly looked away, as if remembering herself.

"Yes," she replied. "We'll start as soon as they arrive." She turned her head toward him but didn't look up. "If you'll excuse me, Mr. Ward, I better go see if Mrs. Werner needs my help with anything."

Peter frowned as she left the room. He was *Mr. Ward* again? "This is hopeless."

"Why Peter, I never knew you to be so faithless," the professor said, checking his pocket watch against the time displayed on the mantel clock.

"I have plenty of faith in God, sir, just not in this plan."

Dr. Kirby snapped shut his watch. "Don't worry. 'All things work together for good to them that love God'." Outside, a carriage pulled up, and he walked to the window. "It's my brother and sister-in-law."

Peter followed the professor to the entrance in the parlor and watched as he opened the door and greeted them. He was relieved to see that Jonah Kirby appeared much more pleasant in person. The stern picture of him from the professor's mantel had haunted him ever since

Dr. Kirby suggested this crazy plan. His wife and Millie, Anne's sister, accompanied him. A lanky young man with a shock of brown hair, who could only be her brother, Jacob, completed the group.

"How are you all, Jonah?" the professor asked, slapping him on the back. "How was your trip?"

"Fine." He handed his coat to his brother. "Are you too high and mighty to hang this up for me?" It must have been an old joke between them, because Dr. Kirby laughed.

"Jonah, don't treat your brother so," Mrs. Kirby said, smiling. She took the coat from the professor, and she and Anne's sister hung their wraps on the coat tree.

"Let me introduce you to someone," Dr. Kirby said and led them over to where Peter stood. "This is Mr. Peter Ward."

Mr. Kirby and his wife seemed startled for a moment.

"How do you do, sir?" Peter held out his hand, glancing at the professor, but Dr. Kirby simply smiled.

Mr. Kirby blinked then took his hand. "I'm well, thank you." He turned to his wife. "This is my wife, Mrs. Adele Kirby."

Mrs. Kirby's eyes were wide as she shook his hand. "I'm pleased to meet you, Mr. Ward."

Dr. Kirby introduced Anne's sister, Millie, and her brother, Jacob. As he finished, Anne came down the hall from the kitchen. She smiled when she saw her family.

"Ma, Pa," she said, hugging each of them. Noticing Peter, her smile faded a fraction. "I see you've met Mr. Ward."

"Yes." Mr. Kirby eyed him carefully and Peter found himself looking at his feet.

"I'm sure he and Jacob will have a lot to discuss this evening," Anne said pointedly. She gave Peter a meaningful, almost pleading, glance before taking her mother's arm. "Mrs. Werner is in the kitchen, Ma. She's eager to meet you and Millie."

"Take Millie with you for now, Anne," Dr. Kirby said. "I need to speak with your ma and pa for a moment."

"Sir," Peter said with rising alarm as the two young women left for the kitchen. "Don't you think—"

"Peter, why don't you take Jacob into the parlor?" Dr. Kirby interjected. "If you recall, he has some questions for you." He led his brother and sister-in-law into the sitting room across the hall and slid the doors shut behind him.

Peter looked at Jacob, who grinned at him.

"Uncle Daniel says you're a horse expert. What do you know about Percherons?"

Unfortunately, Peter knew little about the breed, but he was able to give Jacob a wealth of information about horse care.

"I haven't quite decided whether to commit to raising them," Jacob said. "I've talked to some people at Grange meetings, and now you. I hope to make a decision in the next few months."

"Let me know if I can help again." Peter's gaze wandered to the parlor door. He could just see the closed doors to the sitting room. What were they talking about? Dr. Kirby said this evening would be a surprise for Anne's parents.

"It's sad what happened with Scioto," Jacob said.

"Yes, I wish there had been more I could have done," Peter replied.

"How has my uncle been about it? And my sister? Uncle Daniel's letter to Pa was very brief."

Peter nodded. "They're doing pretty well. I'm sure you couldn't have heard yet about Dr. Townshend's Christmas gift to them." He told Jacob about Spice.

"Dr. Townshend is a good man," Jacob said, smiling broadly.

The sitting room doors opened and Peter swallowed, anticipating the look of disapproval sure to be on Mr. and Mrs. Kirby's faces. After all, he had hardly a penny to his name. How was he supposed to support Anne? But when they came into the parlor, they smiled at him, seeming curiously pleased. He tried to get Dr. Kirby's attention, but the professor ignored him.

"Well, if we are to decorate the tree before dinner, we'd better get started," Dr. Kirby said.

Mrs. Kirby went to the kitchen and gathered Anne, Millie, and Mrs. Werner while Mr. Kirby brought in their box of decorations from the vestibule.

They clipped candleholders onto the branches, strung beads, and tied bows all over the tree. In spite of his nervousness, Peter enjoyed it. Granddad had been generous in his gift giving, but they'd never had a Christmas tree. He reached up to hang a little toy drum and found himself standing very close to Anne. He looked down at her.

"This is my first Christmas with a tree," he said.

She kept her eyes focused on adjusting a string of beads. "Really?"

"Yes, Granddad wasn't quite sure of them. But I had stockings, growing up." Instead of getting another ornament, he continued looking at her. "Has your family always done this?"

"Yes, I think the first one was"—her hands stilled—"the year they adopted me."

Peter glanced behind him. The rest of the family was busy on the other side of the tree. He lifted Anne's chin, forcing her to look at him. "I meant what I said out in the stable, Anne, all of it. He doesn't matter. I love you."

Her eyes darted away from his, and she opened her mouth to say something, but her uncle's voice stopped her.

"Well, I think that looks wonderful," he said.

They all stepped back to look at it. Anne carefully moved away from Peter and stood next to her brother, who smiled down at her and squeezed her shoulders.

Millie cocked her head. "I think I see a bare spot."

"Whether you do or not, it doesn't really matter," her pa said with a smile. "We're out of decorations." He nudged his brother good-naturedly. "You and your big fancy trees."

Dr. Kirby chuckled. "Yes, well why don't we all sit down?"

Everyone took a seat. Peter found himself next to Anne on the sofa. She twisted her hands in her lap.

Mrs. Werner was the only one who hadn't taken a seat. "I'll be going to see about dinner," she said.

"Let me help you," Anne said quickly and started to rise.

"No, lass, you stay with your family. It'll be ready shortly, Dr. Kirby."

Mrs. Kirby looked at her brother-in-law. "Where are Rebecca and Joseph, Daniel? I thought they would be here."

"They'll be here tomorrow. In fact, I have good news from both of them." He rose from his seat, picked up the picture of his children on the mantel, and smiled down at it. Looking at his brother, he said, "I'm sorry to beat you to this, Jonah, but Rebecca wrote to tell me that I should be a grandfather in the spring."

Amid exclamations of happiness, Jonah joined his brother at the mantel and hugged him. Peter glanced at Anne; her smile was strained. His heart ached for her. He fervently hoped the professor's crazy plan worked. Even if it took him his whole life, he was determined to make sure that look never crossed Anne's face again. Dr. Kirby spoke and Peter turned his attention to him.

"As for my news about Joseph—" He took a deep, steadying breath. "As you know, after Katherine passed he felt it would be too hard to stay and attend college here in Ohio." The professor's beard bristled as he pressed his lips together. "But it seems he misses his mother even more keenly living so far away from home. He has decided to attend The Ohio State University, starting next term."

Peter offered his congratulations along with everyone else, but even over the noise, he heard a sigh beside him. He set his jaw. *You'll be here to see him, Anne. With me standing right at your side.* The merriment died down and Dr. Kirby looked at him. If Peter had been nervous and unsure of this before, he wasn't now.

"I have more good news," the professor said. "It concerns a young man whom it has been my pleasure to know for the past several months." Peter felt uncomfortable as Dr. Kirby looked him straight in the eye. "He introduced himself to me as Peter Ward, but I have discovered his real name is Peter Tobias McCord."

Peter felt as if a horse had kicked him in the gut. In a daze, he looked around at them. Dr. Kirby, his brother, and his sister-in-law appeared calm, but the others looked confused, Anne most of all. The mantel clock struck the hour, and a carriage pulled up outside. Silently, the professor left the room. He returned, bringing someone with him. Peter's jaw dropped, and he stood.

"Jimmy!" he exclaimed.

Chapter 17

"Hello, sir." The valet smiled and crossed the parlor to shake Peter's hand. "Actually my name is James Brooks." He glanced at the professor. "I'm a Pinkerton agent."

"What?" Peter exclaimed. "Who were you working for? My uncle?"

Dr. Kirby laid his hand on Peter's shoulder and urged him to sit. "Just listen to him."

Peter looked at the professor as he sat down. "You've heard this, then?"

"Yes. All of it."

Peter pressed his lips together and ran his hands through his hair in frustration. "I never wanted anyone to know," he said angrily. "It was all in the past."

"I had to know who you were for reasons that you don't understand yet. Please hear Mr. Brooks out."

Peter sighed and looked at James.

"Your grandfather hired the agency," James said calmly, "to watch over you."

"To watch over me? Why?"

"He'd been getting death threats."

Peter frowned and stared at James. "He never told me."

"He didn't want to worry you. The threats began years ago, while you were at Princeton, but he never took them seriously until one of them mentioned you. That's when he called us in. He knew you'd never agree to have a bodyguard around all the time, so that's why I posed as your valet."

"He didn't ask for anyone for himself?"

"No, you were his main concern."

"Then his illness—" Peter began.

"Unfortunately the threats were not unfounded," James replied heavily.

Peter worked his jaw. "Who?" he asked, although in his heart, he already knew.

"Your uncle, with the help of your cousin Edward, slowly poisoned him. They also changed his will. Mr. Jamison, your grandfather's lawyer, helped with that." James pulled out some documents from his suit and handed them to Peter. "I found your grandfather's real will. Your uncle, your cousin, and Mr. Jamison have been arrested."

Peter slowly opened the will. It was the exact opposite of the document his uncle had shown him in May. As Granddad had always said, he left Peter nearly everything. An annuity had been set up for Uncle Randall and his family. He understood what had motivated Uncle Randall and Edward. They'd wanted the entire

McCord fortune, not a yearly stipend. But what had motivated Mr. Jamison? Granddad had trusted him explicitly. Letty came to mind and he looked at James. "How does Letty Jamison fit in to all this?"

A scowl crossed James's face. "It seems she did get herself in the family way, but your cousin Edward was responsible. Mr. Jamison took the matter to your uncle, who agreed to have Edward marry her, *if* the attorney changed your grandfather's will."

"But once he'd done it, Edward refused to marry her," Peter said.

"Mr. Jamison threatened to reveal the whole thing unless they provided a husband for his daughter. So they took advantage of your way with the ladies, hoping to trap you into marrying her." James grinned. "You leaving *before* the wedding complicated their plans, but I'm glad you got away."

Peter looked down, wishing James hadn't put it quite like that. What must Anne think of him now?

"What happened to Miss Jamison?" Mrs. Kirby asked.

"After Mr. McCord left, his uncle paid Mr. Jamison to keep quiet, and she was sent away. The child came early, stillborn."

"The poor girl," Mrs. Kirby murmured.

James shrugged. "At least, she didn't get a hold of these." He handed a velvet box to Peter.

"You found them." He opened the box to look at his mother's pearl necklace. He sighed with relief.

"Yes sir, with the note you left me." He reached into his pocket. "I also managed to track down these." He pulled out mother-of-pearl cuff links. "Your trail ended at the pawn shop where I found them."

"That's the last time I bet on a sure thing," Peter said, taking them. He glanced at Dr. Kirby, shame-faced.

"That's who you used to be, Peter. Not who you are now." He nodded to James. "Please give him the let-ter, Mr. Brooks."

Peter looked up at them. "What letter?"

"Your grandfather left a letter for you, sir, to be read when the will was read." James retrieved an envelope from a pocket inside his coat and handed it to him.

"Peter," Dr. Kirby said quietly. "I know this seems like an intrusion, but it's important that you read it out loud."

Peter hesitated, but seeing the sincere entreaty on the professor's face, unfolded the letter and cleared his throat.

Dear Peter,
You are reading this now because I have passed and my legacy is now in your hands. I know that you never were one for business, but I trust your common sense and I am confident you will find an honorable man to run McCord Steel and Iron-works on your behalf.

But that is not the reason I am leaving you this letter. Guilt has a way of lying on a man's heart like a hot steel beam, and such is the case with me. For your whole life, I have kept a secret from you. Coward that I am, I have never been able to tell you, fearing your anger and what you might do when you found out.

As you know, your mother, Sarah, was my only daughter. She was a great source of joy for me, and I wanted nothing but the best for her. I sent her to the finest finishing schools. She was the most popular young lady in Pittsburgh society. But the War Between the States began, and it was then that Sarah strayed from my carefully laid plans for her.

She met a young man by the name of Tobias Kirby, a private in a Union regiment being mustered in Pittsburgh. I do not know the specifics of how they met, but he swept her off her feet. They married secretly after only a few weeks. Eventually, he was sent off for service, and when Sarah discovered she was with child, she revealed to me what she had done.

My anger toward your mother was terrible, even more so when I discovered the Kirbys were no more than farmers in Ohio. I immediately sent her abroad, and when she returned with you, I circulated the story that she had married someone who turned out to be a fortune hunter and divorced her when he discovered he would get no money from me.

By the time you and she arrived back in Pittsburgh, the war was over. Sarah was heartbroken when she learned your father had been killed at Cold Harbor and angry at me for not telling her. We fought, and she left the house only to die in the carriage accident.

*I had nothing left of my daughter but you and,
afraid the Kirbys would come and take you away,
I decided to make sure you never knew about
your father's family. I destroyed the marriage
certificate and Tobias Kirby's effects the Union
Army sent me and told you the same story I told
everyone else.*

*As time went on, I could not remain at peace
with what I had done, and yet I could not find the
courage to tell you the truth. I have since learned
the Kirbys are good people, people I should not
have been ashamed to call my relations. I am
ashamed of my actions and I can only pray that
you, they, and God can forgive me.*

> *I remain your loving grandfather,*
> *Hiram C. McCord*

A second sheet of paper listed the address of the
Kirby farm in Delaware. Peter let them both fall to the
floor as he lifted incredulous eyes to the professor, who
now stood beside his brother in front of the mantel.
"This is why you had to find out who I was?" he asked.

The professor nodded. "Toby was our brother," he
said, his voice thick with emotion. "When Jonah and
I left to fight the war, he was supposed to have stayed
behind at the farm to help Ma run the farm. But he
always was a headstrong young man. I guess the call
to serve wouldn't leave him alone, and he ran off and
joined up. Why he went clear to Pennsylvania, I guess
we'll never know."

Peter stood up and walked over to them. "But what made you think I was his son?"

"Your eyes," the professor replied. "You woke up and looked at me with those eyes of yours."

Confused, Peter looked from him to his brother. Both of them gazed steadily at him and that was when he saw it—two sets of eyes exactly like his own, as green as a spring meadow.

"I wasn't positive until I finally got you to shave that beard of yours," Dr. Kirby said.

"You look just like him," Mr. Kirby added.

The two embraced him, and Peter felt awestruck that of all the people he could have come across during his days of wandering, the Lord led him to his own family and restored him to them. Dr. Kirby—Uncle Daniel—pulled away and gave his shoulder a squeeze. "There is one more thing you're forgetting," he said, nodding toward where Anne sat on the sofa.

Peter started then looked at Jonah. He smiled. "It's not like you're related by blood," he said quietly.

Swallowing, he looked at Anne. She stared at him with saucer-like eyes. Spying the velvet box that contained his mother's pearls lying on the sofa next to her, he picked them up and sat down, facing her. He opened the box, revealing the pearls.

"These belonged to my mother," Peter said. "I'd be very happy if you wore them on our wedding day."

He saw the shock in her eyes for only a moment before she fled the room.

Anne shut herself in the sitting room. The news of Peter's wealth and his true identity had been startling enough, but his proposal left her completely undone. Ever since they'd kissed, she'd fought between running straight into Peter's arms and telling him everything to leaving in the middle of the night. She shook her head, trying to clear it, and as she did so, the doors to the sitting room opened and Peter walked in. He shut them and flashed her one of his most roguish smiles.

"You left before answering my question."

Anne stared at him. "I can't marry you, Peter. I can't marry anyone."

He took her by the arms. "That's ridiculous. Of course you can. You can marry me."

"No, my father—"

"I told you I don't care about his condition."

"You should." Anne pulled away and stood by the window, her back to him. "He's not just lost his senses, Peter. He's a murderer." She held her breath, waiting for the sound of the sitting room doors opening and Peter walking out the front door.

"I know."

She whirled around, certain she hadn't heard right. "You know? But—but how?"

He walked over to her. Reaching into the breast pocket of his jacket, he pulled out two letters and held them up in front of her. "I found these in Spice's stall."

She stared at the letters then took them from his hand. With everything that had happened, she'd never realized they were gone.

"I showed them to Uncle Daniel, and he told me everything. Your father wasn't in his right mind when he killed your mother and your pa's neighbor." He pulled her into his arms. "You've been running down the wrong path, Anne. God wants to lead you to green pastures and beside still waters. And if you search your heart, I think you'll find me right there alongside you."

Anne thought she couldn't stand the joy she felt as she finally let into her heart what God had been trying to tell her for so long. But it was quickly tempered by her next thought, and she raised apprehensive eyes to his.

"What if someone finds out about my father?"

His face hardened a little. "No one is going to find out. I'll bankrupt McCord Steel if I have to."

The relief she felt was so intense she laid her head on his chest.

"So you'll marry me?" he whispered into her hair.

Anne raised her head. Unable to resist, she gave him a roguish smile of her own. "Are you sure you know what you're getting into? I can't cook, I can't sew, and I'd rather be in a stable than the kitchen—"

Anne's words were stopped by a kiss that she returned fully with a restored heart.

* * * * *

Author's Note

Scioto's care and treatment mentioned in these pages is drawn from *Magner's Classic Encyclopedia of the Horse*, originally published in 1887. I apologize for any errors made regarding horse care in the nineteenth century. It was purely unintentional.

At the time of this story what most Ohio State students and alumni now call University Hall was known as the Main Building, and Mirror Lake was simply called "the Lake." To see the dramatic changes that have taken place on the university campus from 1871 to the present, I encourage you to visit The Ohio State University Interactive Historical Campus Map at knowlton.osu.edu/historymap as well as the John H. Herrick Archives at herrick.knowlton.ohio-state.edu.

O–H–I–O!

REQUEST YOUR FREE BOOKS!

2 FREE CHRISTIAN NOVELS
PLUS 2
FREE
MYSTERY GIFTS

HEARTSONG
PRESENTS

YES! Please send me 2 Free Heartsong Presents novels and my 2 FREE mystery gifts (gifts are worth about $10). After receiving them, if I don't wish to receive any more books I can return the shipping statement marked "cancel." If I don't cancel, I will receive 4 brand-new novels every month and be billed just $4.24 per book. That's a savings of 20% off the cover price. It's quite a bargain! Shipping and handling is just 50¢ per book in the U.S.* I understand that accepting the 2 free books and gifts places me under no obligation to buy anything. I can always return a shipment and cancel at any time. Even if I never buy another book, the two free books and gifts are mine to keep forever.

159 HDN FT97

Name _____ (PLEASE PRINT) _____

Address _____ Apt. # _____

City _____ State _____ Zip _____

Signature (if under 18, a parent or guardian must sign)

Mail to the **Reader Service:**
IN U.S.A.: P.O. Box 1867, Buffalo, NY 14240-1867

Not valid for current subscribers to Heartsong Presents books.

* Terms and prices subject to change without notice. Prices do not include applicable taxes. Sales tax applicable in N.Y. This offer is limited to one order per household. All orders subject to credit approval. Credit or debit balances in a customer's account(s) may be offset by any other outstanding balance owed by or to the customer. Please allow 4 to 6 weeks for delivery. Offer available while quantities last. Offer valid only in the U.S.

Your Privacy—The Reader Service is committed to protecting your privacy. Our Privacy Policy is available online at www.ReaderService.com or upon request from the Reader Service.

We make a portion of our mailing list available to reputable third parties that offer products we believe may interest you. If you prefer that we not exchange your name with third parties, or if you wish to clarify or modify your communication preferences, please visit us at www.ReaderService.com/consumerchoice or write to us at Reader Service Preference Service, P.O. Box 9062, Buffalo, NY 14269. Include your complete name and address.